"PREVIEW"

[A Wholesome, Metaphysical, Religious Comedy, Offering
Humor and Comfort To The Unanswered Question-"What Happens
To People Before They Die?"]

A unique, warm relationship develops when Solly, our hero,
takes Rabbi "Goyshan", (Formally a Guru) under his
protection, (Who's protecting who?) during one of Solly's
non-Snowbird trips to Miami Beach, Florida.

Solly is not your typical "Snowbird"! Solly really dislikes
them. In his mind he sets himself apart from them. He
travels with them, but that's it! He is not running away
from the freezing temperatures and snow. He is traveling
south for only one reason. He is lonely, and yearns to
spend as much time as possible, with his loving daughter,
"Kimberly Tara", and with his affectionate mother "Molly".

While under the influence of too many screwdrivers, Goyshan
reveals to Solly, his High Lama's concept of how people
cross-over into the next world. Each person "crosses over"
in a split second, without any pain or suffering. At
exactly this moment their Cross-Over Angel takes over their
body,becomes their surrgogate, and remains until their
bodies must leave this world. Solly doesn't buy this
"Bubba Meiser" (Grandmother's fairy tale.) Goyshan, still
under the influence, reveals to Solly that
"sometimes","sometimes"a novice Cross-Over Angel messes up,
maybe… one in a million cross-overs, through negligence or
inexperience, and their identity becomes questioned. Many
Cross-Over Angels have permission to fake Alzheimer's. This
way they get away with not having to remember too much
about their target's history.
[Later on in our screenplay, Solly comes face to face with
his own mother's crossover! This was one of those-one in a
million mess ups! Solly and Goyshan witness this mind
shattering, soul searching, event in disbelief.Can Solly
adapt? Will Solly survive his realization that he too, will
cross-over some day? Will Solly take on the yoke of his
religion's commandments and statutes, so that at the end,
he will go up, not down?]

Solly's reaction to Goyshan's secret, is that Goyshan is
"doozie-batz"! "Crazy" in Italian.
At the end of their flight to Florida, Goyshan thought that
he was flying to Florida for acupuncture, but his ticket's

1

final destination read "Acapulco". (Mexico)
Had Solly not intervened, Goyshan would have ended up in
Acapulco, Mexico.
After Solly realizes Goyshan's vulnerability and naivety,
he takes him under his wing, brings him to Molly's
apartment, and introduces him as "Rabbi Goyshan".
[The groundwork is set, for Solly's future discovery, when
Molly plays her piano for him and Goyshan, that she has
crossed-over! Whenever she plays the piece "Poems", at a
certain point, she always hits the wrong keys and must
replay. It is very annoying to whoever is listening. This
time, Molly plays it perfect! Solly's suspicians are
correct! His mother has crossed-over,and her body is
occupied by an angel]
Goyshan meets Kimmy, Solly's daughter, at the Kosher,
Mosher, Peking restaurant. He is captivated by her. He also
meets hot Chinese mustard for the first time.

Again, Solly is heart broken when he leaves Kimmy and his
mom. Solly and Goyshan return to Solly's home, on beautiful
White Lake, New York, where he has a boat, seaplane and jet
ski rental business. He is constantly thinking about Kimmy,
and how he can spend more time with her before she gets all
grown up.
Solly's distraction from all this pain is his playing and
writing country music. He has even entered a local song
writing contest with his new song, "Mountain Man". (Solly
is the "Mountain Man" because he lives in the Catskill
Mountains.)
Solly's inner conflict has become more complex since his
last trip to Florida. Should he try to live a more
religious way of life, learn the intricacies of the Torah
so that he can pass his new Torah knowledge onto his
daughter Kimmy? Is his cross-over angel close at hand or
maybe, right around the corner?

Solly reaches out to his neighbor Rabbi Fishbone for
answers. It is at this meeting that Rabbi Fishbone asks
Solly for his help to raise money to renovate the synagogue
before the oncoming High Holydays.

The ten Rabbis who are the Board of Directors of the
Synagogue unanimously approve Solly's idea to have a "WLO".
White Lake Olympics.(Only after Solly explained that "WLO"
has nothing to do with the "PLO".)

Now, on the radio, and TV, "Be in the grandstands to watch and cheer-on our ten local Rabbis while they compete against each other during the White Lake Olympics. Exciting! Hilarious competition! Enjoy the exciting swimming competition, speed boat races, jet ski races, and water skiing races. Hang onto your beards, Rabbis, and let the races begin! Don't miss the WLO! WLO means...... White, Lake, Olympics! There will also be an opportunity to bet, no, I mean donate, and be a winner. It's all for a good cause. Be there! August 6th, at White Lake New York, highway 17B."

(The aqua sports will be reminiscent and resemble the old black and white silent movie action races, with our Rabbis wearing the long sleeved, long legged, striped bathing suits, of the 1920's and 1930's. To accentuate the flashback, old look, we will intermittently shift between color and black and white.)

Can betting windows, called "Donation Booths" get around the state gambling regulations? The Indian tribes have been trying to get gambling approved in Sullivan County for thirty years with no success. Can ten Rabbis get it done in three weeks? Will their prayers help raise renovation dollars?

Just before the races begin, three local hoodlums grab one of the Rabbis and take his number and substitute their entry. This guy is built like Schwarzenegger and is sure to win all the races and money. They are sure to bankrupt the synagogue, but Solly and Goyshan, who are also contestants, vow that this gangster is not going to win! They team up to stop him.

Will the WLO be a money maker, or a disaster?

Solly's daughter Kimmy (about ten years old), doesn't have the emotional strength of her father, to be separated by distance, and runs away from home. She wants to be a real "Snowbird", and heads north on a Greyhound, to White Lake New York, to be with her daddy. Solly is horrified by her actions, but is secretly thrilled. Until Kimmy safely arrives at the N.Y.C. Port Authority, the whole family is a nervous wreck.

It is not everyday that a ten year old makes a fifteen hundred mile bus trip alone.

Kimmy arrives just in time for the Jewish Holydays. With the help of Rabbi Fishbone and his daughter Rivkah, (same age as Kimmy) Kimmy learns all about the Holydays.

Solly learns about the commandment to "Take the four species" to make a Luluv,and the commandment to "Dwell in Booths." (Succahs)
Rabbi Goyshan, with the help of Rabbi Gross,(a small person)after two attempts,build a "Succah". It is large enough for the whole Batimo family to sing and dance in. We learn what a Luluv is, and the important part it plays in the Holiday of Succos.
Solly purchases Luluvs for himself, Goyshan, Molly, Julie, and Kimmy, at a nearby Succah factory. (We capture and show the entire "Essence" and "Joy" of this holiday, Succos.)
Julie and Kimmy return to Florida, but Molly remains in Solly's house.
THEN IT HAPPENS!
While Molly is playing her piano, she plays her favorite piece "Poems" PERFECTLY! The absence of fumbling, and hitting the wrong keys, at a certain bar of the music, as she has always done before, tips off Solly and Goyshan that she is an "Angel" and has crossed over.

Solly cries out.. " My mother is an Angel!"
Goyshan quickly covers Solly's mouth with his hand.

There is a complete change in Solly's personality and gruff responses to Molly. Solly realizes that he should be more sensitive to her and only be on his best behavior. It's not everyday that one has an Angel to take care of!
Solly also doesn't want to have a bad relationship with a an angel, who has the ability to remove someone out of this world into the next, in a split second.

Molly convinces Solly that she would be happier living in the nearby nursing home. "Solly, do you know that they have a "Grand" piano at the White Lake Nursing Home?" (This was a relief to him, because of the emotional pressure that he had built up, having to deal everyday with an Angel.)

Goyshan and Solly move Molly to the nursing home. As soon as she arrives she rushes to the large auditorium to sit down to play the Grand piano.
Solly and Goyshan are both very happy that Molly is happy.
Solly kisses Molly goodbye.
Solly (to himself) "I can't believe it was an Angel, who I just kissed! Come to think of it,…Molly was always an Angel!"

4

The following evening Solly drives to visit Molly, to see
how she has settled in.
As he approaches the building he hears a symphony playing.
After going through the main doors, he walks down the
hallway toward the direction of the music.
The music gets louder and louder, as Solly approaches the
main auditorium. The hallway upon which Solly is walking is
very dark. As he approaches the auditorium door, it is
slightly ajar, and a very strong white light is shining
through. The music continues to get louder and even more
beautiful. They are playing "Poems"! Solly's favorite.
Upon entering the large room Solly sees over a hundred
senior citizen musicians, all playing together, or maybe a
hundred "Cross-Over Angels"?
Solly spots Molly at the piano. He then scans the rest of
the musicians, all dressed in <u>white</u> formal attire. This all
white scene sends a glaring white glow throughout the
auditorium. There is a large glass skylight through which
the light is concentrated and shining up and passing
through.

<u>Black Screen</u>-Large White Letters "Please do not tell your
friends about our surprise ending!"
Close-up on Solly and Goyshan with their fingers to their
lips.

—

SNOWBIRDS

By

George H. Gisser

AUTHOR'S INTRODUCTION

This screenplay is a FICTIONAL works, not to be interpreted to have been derived from the Torah, (Old Testament).

When Moses received the Torah from G-D, on Mount Sinai, he was instructed to command the Jewish Nation "Not to add nor subtract even one letter from this original Bible."

My screenplay does not pertain to any commandment or Torah concept. Any implication to the opposite is not my intent .My sole intent is to offer a "Wouldn't it be nice if the following fictional concept would be true"

Since Judaism is a "Religion of Logic", I have used my logic and imagination to answer the questions of "How did G-D allow the tragedies of World War Two, to happen?" Many modern day Rabbis have unsatisfactually answered their constituents with.."Don't go there!" or-"G-D works in mysterious ways!" or-"Don't ask! When G-D wants us to know, He will tell us!"

My answer is this FICTIONAL "Wouldn't it be nice" screenplay. "Snowbirds" offers a logical answer, even though the cross-over angel concept is a fantasy. On the positive side...our screenplay provides people a wholesome theoretical answer to life's sufferings. We should utilize our lives to prepare our souls for the "World to Come"and not be caught in the quicksand of doubts and confusion.

Too many people have turned away from G-D because no one has offered a logical explaination to their unanswered questions.

Hopefully, "Snowbirds" will show how G-D is a good G-D,WHO has brought man into this world painlessly, and will bring him into the"World to Come" painlessly.

The cross-over angel concept opens many humorous possibilities, so sit back and enjoy, retaining the thought-"Wouldn't that be nice!"

OUR FILM BEGINS........

White Lake, New York-Autumn

Location: (White Lake, New York)

Camera: (Aerial view) (Around November first, we pan on the beautiful lake, White Lake, of Sullivan County, New York. We are viewing the lake through the eyes of a bird. The bird swoops down and skims the water.)

Action: Jeffery and his wife Sandra, are walking towards their Recreational Vehicle.

Camera: (Close-up)

JEFFERY
Come on, come on already! It's almost nine o'clock! You know I like to leave early to get a head start on the traffic. If it were up to me we would have left at six. I want to be in Florida by Friday.
(Sarcastically)If it were up to me, we would be getting on the plane, right now at Newark! (Sing-song) But you don't like to feel the pressure on your dainty ears.

SANDRA
Jeffery, you know I need to pack more stuff than you. I've forgotten something! Oh, yes, did you take my winter coat? You know it can get very cold in Florida. Before I set one foot in your R.V., you have to show me my winter coat!

JEFFERY
No one takes a winter coat to Florida, (pause) but you're the boss! I'm going back into the house to get it.

CAMERA
(Back shot on Jeffery going into the house, pan onto Sandra, sitting in the passenger seat of R.V., putting on lipstick. We then pan back to Jeffery coming out of the house, carrying Sandra's coat.)

JEFFERY
(Talking to himself) Let's see,…everything turned
off, garbage out on the curb, yeah, that does it.
(He locks the door, turns around and enters the
vehicle.) Here's your coat!

SANDRA
(Takes the coat and takes it to the rear, where
she hangs it in a closet. She turns around and
comes up front, then sits down next to Jeffery.)
Wait! Before we start… (Opens the door, then
steps out of the R.V.)… I have to use the ladies
room. (Sandra walks around to Jeffery's window,
and extends her hand.)
Can I have the keys?

JEFFERY
(Thinking for a moment, to himself, then blurts
out.)
I think I left them in the house!

SANDRA
(Getting annoyed, and raising her voice.)
What did you do that for? I've got to go to the
bathroom!

JEFFERY
I left them in the house, (trying to cover his
mistake) because we won't need them until next
Spring when we come back! (Also raising his voice
defensively, and matter of fact.)

SANDRA
(Screaming) How are we going to get into the
house next Spring? Get out of the R.V., and open
the door!

JEFFERY
(Gets out of the vehicle and walks over to the
door)
(Thinking) Next Spring I was going to use the
spare keys! Spare keys! That's it!

SANDRA
(She snaps the keys away from Jeffery, and goes
into the house)

        JEFFERY
(Goes back into the R.V.)

        SANDRA
(Finally comes out, gets into the R.V. and closes
the door.)
Let's go!

        JEFFERY
(Starts up the engine)
Where are the keys? Please give them to me!

        SANDRA
(Close-up on her face. Meekly, and in a low
voice)
(Her mouth falls open, and a surprise look comes
over her face.)
I left them with your keys!

        CAMERA
(Leaves the interior of the R.V., then we pan an
aerial view of the top of the vehicle, going
higher and higher, then showing the vehicle
leaving the curb and driving away.)

        OFF-STAGE
(Jeffery's voice)
(Annoyed, and raising his voice.)
How are we going to get into the house next
Spring? How could we be so stupid?

(Sandra's voice)
Look who's calling me Stupid! Who left the first
set of keys in the house?

(Jeffery's voice)
That's different! When I did it, we had a spare
set over the door. (yelling) and when I called
you stupid, I was being nice to you!

(Sandra's voice)
You haven't been nice to me for thirty years!

        SOUND
(Sandra turned the radio on to drown-out
Jeffery.)

OFF-STAGE
(Jeffery's voice)
I'll never make it to Florida, cooped up with
you! I should have taken the plane!

Cut to Jeffery pulling up Solly's driveway.
Yelling from his vehicle.

        SOLLY
(Dressed in country-western clothes.)
(Covering up boats in his yard.)

        JEFFERY
Well, we're finally off! Solly, could you keep an
eye on my house this winter?

        SANDRA
(Disparaging) and if there is a problem, you
won't be able to get into the house! Big mouth,
here, locked the keys in the kitchen!

        SOLLY
Then how do I get into the house?

        SANDRA
(Really enjoying this put down of Jeffery)
You will just have to call the police! (Laughing)

        JEFFERY
Thank you Solly. Maybe we will see you in
Florida.

        SOLLY
So long you two love birds. Have a safe trip!
(Waves goodbye.)

        SOUND
(Music in the vehicle gets louder. We make a
sound transition, from the radio in vehicle to
Solly's radio on his deck.)

        CAMERA
(Pan from radio to Solly, who is continuing his
work.)

        GARAGE INT.

He then goes into the garage and cavers up more boats

OFF-STAGE

          RADIO ANNOUNCER
Welcome to mountain country! Welcome to the Catskill Mountains! Station 97.9 VOS. Before I star spinning country songs, let me remind you that the last entry date for your music will be in two weeks from today. So, mail them in and maybe your song will win you and yours, a free trip to Nashville and five hundred dollars. Write down this mailing address: Country Creations, P.O. Box 234, Monticello, NY 12701. Good luck, and now back to that old favorite by Johnny Cash, "I'll Walk the Line" (Music fades in).

          SOLLY
I'm going to win that contest!
(Talking to himself) Another season! I hope this coming winter will be easy. Maybe only 2-3 feet of snow.

          OFF-STAGE
(Telephone ringing)

          GARAGE EXT.
          CAMERA
(Solly puts the lock on the garage doors. He leaves the garage and goes onto his house to answer the phone.)

(This scene is inside Solly's kitchen.)

          MAX
(Calling from Florida.)
(Close-up on Max)

(Overlapping man's voice) (Telephone conversation.)

Hello, hello, Solly, this is your cousin, Max. Do you know what's going on down here? Your mother has the whole family tied up in knots! She won't come to the funeral! You gotta do something fast!

We are saying goodbye to Nat tomorrow afternoon.
See you at the funeral!
(Hang up sound.)

[Switch back to close-up on Solly]

        SOLLY
Good-bye.

        SOLLY
(Calls up Molly.)
(Voice on the phone.)
(Visual is close-up on Molly in
Florida)(Irritated)

        MOLLY
Your father was no good! He was a drunk, a horse
player, a very selfish man. No way am I going to
his funeral! A gonif (crook), too! Do you know
how many times I caught him going to my bag?
That's final! Good-bye! (switch back to close-up
in Solly)

        SOLLY
(In a low voice) Good-bye.

        CAMERA
(Close-up on a very sad Solly.)

(Solly picks up his guitar on his way back out to
the dock, shuts off the radio and commences to
play his guitar.)

Close-up on Kimmy's picture on deck table.Solly
is singing to her, and for her.

        SOLLY
I'm going to win that contest! (Sings the
following country song.)

        SOLLY
Is there a girl down there
     Awaitin down there,
Who'll start for me
     A brand new life?

Maybe there's a girl down there

Awaitin down there,
Who'll come and be my wife?
I'm a Mountain Man,
    A shoutin man,
Who's tired of this lonely life

Maybe there's a girl down there
    Awaitin down there
Who'll come and be my wife?

Maybe I've been holed up here,
    Frozen up here,
Crazy from the snow.

Maybe there's a girl down there,
    Awaitin down there,
Who I should get to know.

I'm a Mountain Man,
    A shoutin man,
A God fearing man.

Who's been holed up here for too long,
    You can tell how lonely I feel
By listening to this song.

I'm a Mountain Man,
    A shoutin man,
Who loves this crisp blue sky.

But I need a warm woman,
    Before I go and die.

I'm a Mountain Man,
    A shoutin man,
I'm a countin man for sure,
    She knows I'm soon to come,

But when I marry her,
    My mountain days are done.

(After Solly finishes his song, there is a pause
with complete silence.)

(The camera captures the peaceful calm of the
lake; when all of the sudden the camera and sound
startles us)

OFF-STAGE
Cut to: (Very, very loud sound of the motors of
three jet skis).

(Camera picks up the skyward shooting of water
from ski jet whizzing by, right in front of
Solly's dock, splashing Solly with a stream of
water. Three bullies are on ski jets and are
making circles, buzzing Solly's dock!)

        BULLY #1
(Close-up)
Common, let's buzz him again!

        BULLY #2
Did you see his face? (Laughing)

        BULLY #3
We really got him pissed!

        SOLLY
(Waving his fist in the air.)
You'll get yours!

(Scene fades out on the three ski jets speeding
away on the lake.) FADE OUT

Cut to (Fade in to Kennedy airport departure
scene N.Y.)

        BACKGROUND INFO
Molly Batimo lives in Miami Beach, Florida. Solly
Botimo lives in White Lake, New York, Solly is a
self-imposed Snow Bird. Why?

Because every three months Solly flies down to
Miami Beach to visit his mother and daughter.
Each trip has been very trying because of his
mother's abusive ways, especially her stories of
how each of her relatives has done her wrong,
including Solly's father (deceased). Also it is
very difficult emotionally for Solly to leave his
daughter, Kimmy, with his ex-wife, Julie. Solly
loves Kimmy very deeply and is constantly
thinking of her. This trip, Solly is flying down

to his father's funeral. He is not a happy Snow Bird.

There are big problems because his mother doesn't want to go to the funeral. She's been separated from Nat for four years. Nat loved the horses! Solly has a difficult trip ahead.

CAMERA (EXTERIOR)

The taxi pulls up to the curb at Kennedy in front of Carnival Airlines.

SOLLY
(Solly gets out, is handed his luggage, he tips the driver and walks into the terminal.

Solly is standing in line with mostly senior citizens. They are all wearing flowery, bright Hawaiian short sleeved shirts. He stands out because he is wearing a dark brown suit with shirt and tie. They are all jovial and happy and Solly's face expresses a man with the weight of the world on his face.)

SOLLY
(Thinking to himself) Snow Birds! (With disgust)

YENTA
(Seventy year old, short Jewish woman.)
Hi! Are you a Snow Bird? (Before Solly can answer.) Are you married? Tell me, are you Jewish?

SOLLY
(Very nasty in order to disengage any conversation) The answers to your three questions are… NO!(Each No!gets louder than the previous.) NO! NO!
(Solly turns his back on her)

YENTA
Vots eating him? He's not a very nice Snow Bird. (Fades out).

(Shot of the jet taking off)

CUT TO: (SCENE - Inside of Airplane)

          SOLLY
(Close-up on Solly, sitting next to the window.
Takes a swallow from his drink and then finishes
it. He puts on the headphones) (Sound-we hear
Solly switching channels then it remains on the
classical music channel, playing "Poems".)

(Camera pans on passengers with all being white-
haired men and women.)

(Solly is sitting next to the window (in the jet)
and is on his third scotch, when our Yenta
yelling loud at the stewardess drops her magazine
on the floor next to a Garu who is sitting to the
left of Solly.)

(The Garu picks up the magazine for Yenta and
hands it to her.)

          YENTA
Oh, thank you. You're a very kind man. Are you a
Snow Bird?

          GARU
(Dumb look on his face)
What's a Snow Bird?

          YENTA
I'm a Snow Bird! Almost everyone on this plane is
a Snow Bird! That's someone who hates the cold
weather up North and flies South to enjoy the
warm weather in Florida until the Springtime.
Then they go North again. (Matter of fact tone in
her voice.)
Tell me, are you married?

          GARU
(Moves his head left to right)
No!

          YENTA
Are you Jewish?

17

GARU
(Doesn't answer, but has a look on his face,
reacting to Yenta's stupid question. Then points
to the turban on top of his head. We then pan to
Solly.)

SOLLY
(Shot of Solly in front of the window, then
passes by him. Solly closes his eyes, smiles and
nods off and out onto the beautiful blue, white
clouded sky.) (Music-Poems continue).

CUT To: (Aerial view of white cranes, migrating
south. Thousands of beautiful white birds fill
the camera's eye.)

TITLES

Special Effects
Titles come on superimposed on the birds in
flight (Music continues)

(After the titles finish, we slow the motion down
still on the birds to slow motion and then we un-
focus.

After a few seconds, we see un-focus, what looks
like white birds with their wings, flapping very
slowly, but then we focus in on hundreds of white
haired senior citizens all lined up wearing white
sweatshirts, doing calisthenics in slow motion,
with their arms extended imitating the flapping
of the birds wings. This continues for about one
minute.

We go into un-focus again then come back into
focus on the birds in flight. We then pan from
the birds to blue sky and CUT TO outside shot of
Solly's window, showing Solly's face up against
his window, then into the airplane.)

YENTA
(This time she makes believe she accidentally

drops her bag onto the isle between the Garu and
her.) Oops!

          GARU
(Tries to reach Yenta's handbag, but looses his
balance, and falls into the isle knocking over
his tray. He lays there for a moment, gets up and
hands Yenta her handbag.)

          SOLLY
(Wakes up from the commotion made by Garu falling
into the isle. Garu returns to his seat.)

(Front view on Solly and Garu)

          SOLLY
You're alright. You could have left it for the
stewardess to pick up. Can I buy you a drink?

          GARU
Oh, no thank you. We do not indulge in alcohol.

          SOLLY
Common, loosen up. You'll enjoy the trip.

          GARU
Well...O.K.

          SOLLY
Stewardess, please give my friend (secretly into
the stewardess' ear), (a double screwdriver,) and
I'll take a double scotch and a large orange
juice for my friend!

(The stewardess brings the drinks and serves them
and then leaves)

          GARU
This orange juice is very nice, yes,... very nice.
(Starts to get a little tipsy).

Tell me, Solly... Why are you going to Florida? Are
you a Snow Bird?

SOLLY

Me a Snow Bird? Nah - I'm just flying down to
Florida for a funeral. My old man finally bit the
dust.

GARU

Oh, I'm terribly sorry.

SOLLY

(Under his breath) So is his bookie.

GARU

(Drinking more). Having someone close, like a
family member, departing, or as we say, "crossing
over" shouldn't be a sad occasion.

SOLLY

How's that?

GARU

(Secretly)What I'm about to tell you is very
confidential! We believe, in our sect, taught to
us by the high Lama, that when a person crosses
over, to the other side , it is a beautiful time
of eternal change.

SOLLY

What do you mean, "beautiful time"?

My old man suffered for eight years with stomach
ulcers, then it turned to cancer. His stomach was
burning the hell out of him until he croaked.

GARU

That's what it seemed to you! (Smiling) [Now
weaving back and forth from the alcohol].

SOLLY

What do you mean, <u>seemed</u> to me?

GARU

You see… he didn't feel any pain!

SOLLY

You're crazy!

GARU

No! no! no! Crossing over is painless!

SOLLY

Then what was my old man moaning about during his last two years?

GARU

That wasn't your father! (Pause) You think it was your father! (Pause) He looked like your father! He sounded like your father! But, it wasn't your father! It was his cross-over angel!

SOLLY

[Sitting up, straight, in his seat] An angel? Gimme a break!

GARU

Let me explain. We believe that crossing over is just like being born.
[Pointing his finger at Solly] Do you remember being born?

SOLLY

...No? [Questioned look on his face.]

GARU

Do you remember the doctor slapping you on the fanny the moment you were delivered? (Pause) Of course not!

Being born was painless, and crossing over into the next world is painless.

Why? We believe that the Lord is merciful and kind. He brings us into this world without pain, and removes us without pain, because he is a good G-d, and he is with every generation.

SOLLY

How do you figure my father had no pain?

GARU

Your father had no pain because your father crossed over way before his pain began.
His cross-over angel stepped in, at the appointed time, and was your father's substitute.

SOLLY

You mean when everyone dies, it is not that person, but a cross-over angel?

          GARU
Right! Right! Right! Now you are beginning to understand. You see, your cross-over angel is with you your whole life. For your whole life, he is watching over you. Watching you. Studying you. Learning your every behavior. How you walk, talk, laugh and cry. By the time we are ready to cross-over, he is ready to be your super substitute.

          The Lord is a good G-d. He brings us into this world gently, and removes us gently.

          SOLLY
Here have another drink! (yells) I mean orange juice! Stewardess!

          STEWARDESS
Oh how nice. The two of you are becoming acquainted.

          GARU
[He displays his conditioned reflex to music. Whenever he hears music, he removes a baton from his inside pocket,which is inside a very special velvet case, and proceeds to conduct his imaginary orchestra.(Maybe this baton has extra special qualities? Find out at end of movie)

Garu picks up his earphones, places them on his head, and starts moving his hands, like a symphony conductor to the music. He then takes the stirrer from Solly's glass and stands up, then starts to conduct his orchestra with much enthusiasm with a baton in each hand.

As he moves away from his seat, the earphones become unplugged, and now Garu can't hear anything. He reacts very disturbed, looking around to see who did this naughty thing to him. After a few seconds he realizes what actually happened, reels in the hanging wires, and smiles at his own stupidity.

He then returns to his seat, next to Solly. He
returns the stirrer to Solly's glass, which
happens to be next to Solly's mouth, almost
poking Solly in the eye. Acting very coy, he
removes the earphones from his head.]

        SOLLY
Another round, please!
[Makes finger motion near his head. Indicating
craziness.]
Doozie Batz!

        GARU
[Spreading out over his seat, and partially onto
Solly.]
Can you keep a secret?

        SOLLY
Sure! [Pacifying]

        GARU
Sometimes…[dragging out the word "sometimes"]
[nodding his head up and down]…sometimes…

        SOLLY
Yes, yes, sometimes what?

        GARU
[With a twitch of his head he changes the
subject]

You know Alzheimer's?
These people have already crossed-over!
Lazy cross-over angels have concocted this
condition! These angels have figured a way out
how not to get caught! They make believe they
don't remember anyone, or anything. This way they
can't slip up! Get it?

        SOLLY
[Still has a blank look on his face]

        GARU
Sometimes the cross-over angel slips up, after
they have entered their new body, maybe once in a

23

million cross-overs,…there comes along an angel who hasn't done his homework and slips up. He forgets a little habit or trait, or he hasn't studied his person close enough, and if someone in the family, someone close to their loved one, spots this error, they could be tipped off, revealing to them that their loved one is really an angel. So the angels have created Alzheimer's!

You know, within the next five years, one third of the country will be made up of people over age sixty five! The war babies are the reason for this. Our job, my sect, is dedicated to getting the word out, that people shouldn't fear death, but worry about being judged in the next world, where our souls go, up [points up with his thumb] or down [reverses his thumb down]. G-d is the Maker and Creator because He is the One who instilled in us life, at birth, decreed upon us death, and reinstates us among the living in the world to come.

The world to come, is better than this world!

All people should be comforted with this knowledge, that G-d is a good G-d. He brought us into this world painlessly, and will send his cross-over angel to bring us back into the next world painlessly. [Drinks some more and passes out] [Falls back into his seat.]

        SOLLY
[Raises his eyes to ceiling, extends his hands, palms upwards.]

[Talking to the ceiling] Did you ever hear such a story? This guy's a "whacko"!
He better keep away from drinking!

[Solly starts humming his country song]

I'm a mountain man, a shoutin man……

[Fade out on Solly falling asleep.]

O.S. [Sound] Fade in of jet engine reversing.
Cut to: Close up on rear of jet engine.

          GARU
[Wakes up with a start! Hands and arms
flaying!][He was startled by the loud noise of
the jet engines being reversed, when touching
down.]

Camera: [Outside shot of jet touching down]

          GARU
Are we in Miami yet?

          SOLLY
Let me see your tickets!

          GARU
[Hands his tickets over to Solly. Very nervous]

          SOLLY
[Reading the tickets.]
New York to Miami, and then Miami to Acapulco
Your final destination is Acapulco!

          GARU
[Loud.] Oh no! Someone made a big mistake! Oh no!

          SOLLY
[Yelling to the stewardess] You people have made
a big mistake with this guy's tickets! He wanted
to be going to Miami, but his tickets say
"Acapulco" [Hands ticket to stewardess.]

          STEWARDESS
[Studies the tickets.]
Let me see. That's correct! Final destination-
Acapulco!

          GARU
How could this happen? I told the ticket agent I
was going to Miami to get acupuncture, not
Acapulco!

          STEWARDESS
[Harshly] Please sit down Sir, until the plane

comes to a stop!

          GARU
[Sits back down, with a disturbed look on his
face.]

          YENTA
[To Garu] Don't let them push you
around,zatzgeller!(dear friend)

Fade-out:

          [Airport Lobby Scene]

          SOLLY
[Walking away from the arrival area with Garu in
the background still yelling and screaming at the
airline personnel.]
Do you have any relatives in Miami? Any friends?

          GARU
Not Acapulco. Acupuncture! No… No… No friends. No
relatives. [Lowers head sadly]

          SOLLY
Well…take care…,nice to have met you…
[Starts to offer hand for farewell handshake then
stops]
[After waving good-bye to Garu, he walks another
fifty feet and then stops and scratches his head,
moves his head from right to left, moderately
fast. From a distance we see him talking to
himself, going through an internal battle, stops
moving. When he arrives at his internal decision,
he turns around and hurriedly walks back to Garu
and the airline personnel.]

          SOLLY
He's with me! Forget about it! Come on. I'm
taking care of everything!

          GARU
Where are we going? Where are you taking me? Not
Acapulco? Acupuncture!

SOLLY
(Telephone call to Molly.) [Walking toward taxi
stand.]
[On the telephone] Hi mom, it's me, Solly!
MOLLY
Hi, Chutchucolou (Greek affectionate word, used
by Greek Jews from Yanina Greece.) How are you my
darling?

Where are you calling from? Are you here in
Florida? Did you come for the funeral?

SOLLY
(Annoyed) Yeah, mom, I'm at the airport! How are
you feeling, Kalah? (Means-Good.)

MOLLY
When you are here, I'll tell you!

SOLLY
O.K.! O.K.! (Bothered reaction to Molly's
negative reply. Anticipates malcontent by
mother).We will be there in about one hour.

SOLLY
(Talking to himself) I don't think I can handle
this anymore. I must use maximum self-control
with her. How can I make it through this trip?
I'm going to explode, go nuts...

How am I going to get her to Popu's funeral?

MOLLY
Who is we?

SOLLY
Oh, I forgot to tell you. We have a nice guest.
I'm helping this ...Gar...Garabbi...Rabbi. Rabbi.
Goy...Goyshan!
MOLLY
A Rabbi, how nice...
SOLLY
When we get there, you will meet him.
[Hangs up phone].
SOLLY
(To Goyshan)Mom says she looks forward to meeting

you.

        GOYSHAN
[Close-up on face, smiles.]

[Both start walking toward taxi stand, out of the
terminal. They stop at taxi stand.]
    [Solly takes Yamulka out (skull cap) of his
pocket and puts it on. Solly only wears it, for
his mother's sake. Solly knows he should be
wearing it, but his evil inclination,prevents
him.]

        SOLLY
[Pointing to Goyshan's turban]. Listen...that
Turkish towel on your head has got to go. It's
making you very conspicuous.

[Reaches up to grab turban off Goyshan's head,
but Goyshan pulls away].

        GOYSHAN
(Nervous).

Solly, it's, it's our custom [puts hand on head
protectively] to keep our head covered...it's a
respect thing. It's like saying "we acknowledge
that there is a higher being, overlooking us
all."

        SOLLY
[Takes second yamulka out of his pocket, and
hands it to Goyshan. This was Solly's father's
yamulka. Solly carried it around for good luck.]
Here, wear this. It was my father's kipur.

        GOYSHAN
[Takes off turban, and places yamulka on his
head. He then turns around and looks at his
reflection in glass window of airport.]

Not bad...not bad [He likes his new look! He spits
on both of his hands, then uses his hands to
smooth down his hair on both sides. He then
throws his turban into trash basket.]

        CAMERA

28

[Follows turban's trip into trash.]
Fade out: on extreme close up of turbin. Then un-
focus fade-out]

[Trip from Airport to Miami Beach]

Fade in: [Ride to Jewish Towers]

[Outside taxi view of crossway bridge going into
Miami Beach, past Fountain Bleu Hotel, up Collins
Avenue and then stopping at Jewish Towers.
Fictitous name.]

[Inside taxi]
    SOLLY
We are going to visit my mother and then my
daughter, Kimberly
(To himself) (Oh I miss her so much!). Then I'll
help you find your acupuncture doctor.By the way,
why do you need acupuncture?

    GOYSHAN
I can't tell you. It's personal! And after all,
we just met at the airport.

    SOLLY
[Pressing him.] Come on, come on. What's the
secret? We are both grown men!

[Gets into taxi.]

    GOYSHAN
Shush! [Puts his finger to his lips and points to
the female taxi driver.]

    FEMALE DRIVER
Where are we going boys? Highaleah, the dog
track?

    SOLLY
[Annoyed. Reacting to female driver's know-it-all
attitude.] Jewish Towers, in Miami Beach! Do you
know where that is?

    FEMALE DRIVER
Sure, I know where it is.

Camera: [Traveling scenes going to Miami Beach.
On the way, Solly has driver stop at the florist
to purchase a plant for Molly.]

Fade-in: [Taxi pulling up to Jewish Towers
building. Camera pans on large sign on building.
Sign reads "Jewish Towers-Senior Citizen
Residence." Short take of both men walking into
the building. Then into the elevator, but both
have to back out to let a old women in wheel
chair exit.] (Annoyed look on Solly's face) [They
re-enter elevator, the doors close. End of take.]

CAMERA

[Cut to Solly knocking on Molly's door.]

SOLLY
Hello, Mom. It's me Solly! Please open the door.
[Pause. More Knocking]

She's getting more deaf! [In disgust] Each time I
come down to here see her, she gets worse!

[Yelling] Come on! Come on! Come, open the door.

Background: [When Solly visits his mother in
Miami Beach, Florida, we convey a close
relationship between son and mother, however,
Solly's talk is condescending and gruff. He is up
to his eyeballs with Molly's schtick
(personality). Solly stays in his mother's small
apartment. He tries to sleep on her sofa bed,
which kills his back. Molly uses an electric
stove, and there is an antique T.V. in the living
room, which is 80% snow. Molly's enjoyment comes
from playing the piano, and from listening to her
forty year old radio, which is almost all
static.It is so old, Solly swears; once, when he
turned it on, he heard a Jack Benny episode.

When we walk into Molly's apartment, there is a
walk-in closet on the left. Peering into the
closet, we see clothes on the left and right
sides, leading toward the back wall, against
which are three or four fishing rods, complete

with reels, line and hooks attached. Some hooks
have dried up worms on it.]

SOLLY
[Banging very loud.]

MOLLY
{Finally a reply!] I hear you! I'm coming! My
Pasha! (Means Sultan/King, but more
affectionately.) Please hold on!
[Door opens and Molly affectionately greets her
son with a long, warm embrace and kiss.]

SOLLY
[Kisses his mother back.]
[Turns toward Goyshan]
Mom, this is…a…[whispering to Goyshan] remember,
your name is Goyshan!

GOYSHAN
[Whispering something to Solly, but we can't make
it out.]

SOLLY
[To Molly] His name is, [hesitating] <u>Rabbi</u>
[emphasizes] Goyshan!

MOLLY
[Extending her hand to shake] Nice to meet you,
Rabbi Goy…shan.

GOYSHAN
[Starts to offer his right hand, but quickly
retracts it with the left hand. He then puts both
hands behind his back.]
[In a low voice. Trying not to offend Molly] We
Rabbis aren't allowed to shake hands with women.
It's our religious law! Please forgive me!

MOLLY
[To Solly] He seems to be very nice!
[To herself.] There seems to be something very
familiar about him, staring at his head, but I
just can't figure it out. [Not realizing that he
is wearing her deceased husband's yamulka.]

Oh Solly. What took you so long to some down?

[Making a sarcastic joke], Does someone have to
die, for you to come visit me? [Referring to
Nat's funeral.]
You know, you're just like him! I had to beg him
to do something, before he moved his colou.
(Greek for behind)...And don't start on me to go to
the funeral.(Uses the following episode as an
excuse not to go to the funeral.)
  You were there... when he intentionally pushed me
into the pool...

Cut to: [Flash-back Pool Scence]

[Molly is recalling her bad memories of what her
husband, Nat, did to her.]

O.S. Molly's voice talking to Solly.

Zoom in
[Close up on Solly's face] Exasperated look!

          MOLLY

Solly, you were there when your father pushed me
into the pool...

[Flash-back to pool scene]

The family is gathered together at the pool.
Solly's father, Nat is walking next to the pool
with a glass of scotch in his hand. More than a
little tipsy he bends down to pet the family's
large dog. The dog growls, then jumps up at
Solly's father! Nat startled, jumps backward to
get out of the way, and accidentally knocks Molly
into the pool. [Fully dressed]

Scene ends with Solly jumping into the pool to
rescue his mother. Along with other family
members.

Flash forward to Molly's apartment.

          MOLLY
[Forgiving] Oh! Solly. I'm so happy to see you.

Please sit down. Let me make something for you
and the Rabbi to eat. You must both be starved!
I've been saving some blueberry pie for you. I
just made it(Softly, under her breath) two weeks
ago…
[She goes to the refrigerator, and removes the
pie.I'll taste it to see if it is still good.] I
know it's your favorite…Do you remember when we
used to go berry picking at White Lake? Pasha?
You remember darling, don't you?
We lived at the Peltons?
Mmm.[Under her breath] still tastes good!

You know, we could go out to eat, if you'd like.
I haven't had any Chinese food, since you took me
out last time. Maybe you'd like to treat your old
mother again? [Before he could answer.] Solly,
before we go, could you [embarrassed] help me
with that thing on my nose?

Camera: [Close-up on Molly's face, while she is
looking cross-eyed at her nose in mirror.]

I found this fantastic Kosher Chinese restaurant…
[In her hand is a tweezers, and she is stabbing
at the hair on her nose.]
It's called, "Mosher, Kosher Peking!"

            GOYSHAN
[Embarrassed. Picks up a newspaper and hides
behind it.]

            SOLLY
[Annoyed] O.K.! O.K.! Gimme the tweezers!

            MOLLY
[Hands the tweezers to Solly.]
Come over here by the window. The light's much
better!

[Together they take a few steps over to the
window.]

            SOLLY
[He maneuvers to get a good shot at removing the
hair, by putting Molly's head into a wrestling-

33

type head grip. He moves the tweezers into
position above her nose.

Camera: [Close-up]

        SOLLY
O.K.! O.K.!.......Hold still! I see it!
[Inadvertently, Solly is so close to accomplish
this task, that he has his cheek against Molly's
cheek. Still struggling]
        I think I got it! No! [Anger] I don't
have it! Wait, Mom, try not to move!

[Shift camera around to show Molly's face, which
is in bliss, her eyes closing from enjoying
contact with her son. Maybe a few tears rolling
down her cheek.]

        SOLLY
Rabbi Goyshan, maybe you can help.

Come over here and hold mom's head still so I can
grab it with the tweezers.

        GOYSHAN
[Gets in back of Solly and reaches forward,
around Solly squeezing him while he tries to hold
Molly's head still.] (And the three of them are
talking at once.)

        SOLLY
Hold still, hold still, that's it…

        MOLLY
Be careful, Pasha, the tweezers are sharp!

        GOYSHAN
Do you see it? Do you got it?

        SOLLY
No, this is not going to work!
        Rabbi, you sit on the chair. [Solly
grabs a towel and places it on Goyshan's lap.
Then he places Molly's head on Goyshan's lap with
her face facing toward the ceiling.] Now, hold
her head still.

34

                    MOLLY
My back. You're killing my back.

                    SOLLY
That's it. I got it! [Showing Molly the hair in
the tweezers like a trophy.]

[At this point, he accidentally stabs Goyshan.]

                    GOYSHAN
[Grabs cheek with hand and spins around in pain,
and around, moaning.]
Oh, you stabbed me, oh, I'm O.K., it's O.K.

                    MOLLY
Oh, Rabbi, are you O.K.? I'm sorry! It was all my
fault. Oh, you're bleeding.
[Molly takes a tissue and gently pats Goyshan on
injured cheek]

                    GOYSHAN
That's O.K. Thank you, thank you. I'll be
alright.

                    MOLLY
Oh, thank you, both of you. Goyshan, would you
like to come with us to the mall? Solly always
takes me when he comes down here. He knows it's
hard for me to get around, so I let things go
until he comes down. [Molly takes out a pen and
jots down a list.] The first thing we have to do
is buy a new pair of sandals. The strap broke on
my old pair. Then I have a beauty parlor
appointment, and then we can go eat Chinese.
Let's start right away. [The three exit the
apartment door, take the elevator down, and then
grab a taxi outside the building.]

[All three leave Molly's building and take a taxi
to the shopping mall.]

Background info: [The taxi arrives at shopping
mall, to buy Molly a new pair of open-toed
sandals.

Her left toe is deformed due to arthritis, and
requires a size, two sizes bigger than the right

foot.]

          MOLLY
You're walking too fast, Solly. Give me your arm
so I can hang on.

After we buy me the sandals, I made an
appointment with the beauty parlor. It's right
here in the mall. There is this beautician,
Artie. He's so good. He said he will be working
all day today. I hope I don't miss him.

Then after the beauty parlor, it should be supper
time. I would love it, if we could eat Chinese.

You know Solly, I wait for your visit to take me
around. You know I can't get around without you.
When I used to drive, it was much easier. Anyway,
I get to see you and be with you, my Chochucolou.

          SOLLY
(Annoyed) Yeah! Yeah!
Oh, there's the shoe store. Let's stop in.

          GOYSHAN
I'll wait out here!

[Solly helps his mother into the shoe store and
helps her into the chair where she starts to
light up a cigarette.]

          SALESMAN
I'm sorry madam. There is <u>no smoking</u> in this
store!

          SOLLY
Laughs (to himself). Wait till she gets done with
this character.

          MOLLY
Those tan canvas sandals in the window for $18.00
Could you please show them to me?
          SALESMAN
Please allow me to measure your foot.
[Salesman leans down and looks at the left large
toe. Instead of the toe going out straight, it
hooks to the left at almost a 90 degree angle.]

SOLLY

(To himself) He must realize he is in trouble now.

SALESMAN

Madam, your size is 6 ½ wide!

MOLLY

Good! Bring me a 6 ½ wide and also an 8 ½ wide.

SALESMAN

[Returns with two boxes on top of each other.]

MOLLY

Let's try the 6 ½ wide first.

SALESMAN

[He puts on the right foot with no trouble, but is having a rough time trying to get the left shoe on the left foot.]

MOLLY

It's my arthritis. Please, let me try on the 8 ½ wide.

SALESMAN

[Hands Molly the left shoe size 8 ½ wide.]

MOLLY

[Struggles, but manages to get the shoe on.]

Very good! Let me try them out.
[She stands up and walks around a little, then walks over to the mirror, examines her feet, then walks back to the chair.]
O.K., these will be good I'm taking them.

SALESMAN

Madam, you wish to take one shoe from the size 6 ½, and one shoe from the size 8 ½? That's impossible (raising his voice) that's unheard of. We do not break up sets of shoes!!

MOLLY

(Yelling) Nothing is impossible! You can do it! Put one shoe in the window and one shoe on the shelf, for display purposes.

SALESMAN

Madam! Please leave! Please remove yourself from this store! Immediately!

SOLLY

Easy! Easy! Calm down! We are taking both pairs! Please wrap them up.

MOLLY

(Loud) Solly! What are you doing? I just need one pair!

SOLLY

Please keep still, mom, I know what I'm doing.

SALESMAN

That will be $18.00, times two = $36.00, plus tax.

SOLLY

[Pays the salesman and walks out of the store with two boxes of shoes and his mother.]

MOLLY

I need a cigarette! Let's stop on the bench over there for a minute~

Solly, what have you done? I know money is tight for you these days. You shouldn't have purchased two pairs.

SOLLY

I know we purchased two pairs however...we are not going to keep two pairs. We are going to keep only one pair!

MOLLY

How's that? Please explain it to me, my darling! I'm confused.

SOLLY

Well, when we get home, we will make two sets out of these. One set, a size 6 ½ for the right foot, and one size 8 ½ for your left foot! I'll out the other two shoes together, back in the box, and tomorrow I will go back, into the same chain

store in a different nearby mall, return the
shoes and get the refund.

            MOLLY
Oh, Solly, you're so smart! I'm so proud of you.
[After finishing her cigarette, Molly takes pad
out of her pocketbook and crosses out the first
item on her shopping list]
Now let's go to the beauty parlor!

            GOYSHAN
[Goyshan is waiting outside the shoestore,
licking an ice cream cone.]
Non-fattening!

            SOLLY
I have a great idea! Instead of waiting till
tomorrow to return the shoes, we'll do it today!
[Turning to Goyshan.]
[Solly takes one shoe from each box and puts it
into the box before handing it to Goyshan]
Here Goyshan! Take these shoes back into the
store, and ask them for a refund.

            GOYSHAN
[Nervously] I...I can't do that!

            SOLLY
Why not? Don't you want to help Molly? Don't
worry! They didn't see you when I purchased them.

            GOYSHAN
[Trying to hand the box back to Solly.]
[Stuttering] Er.r.r…

            SOLLY
[Solly spins Goyshan around and shoves him
towards the store's entrance.]

            GOYSHAN

Where's the sales slip? [As he passes through the
doors.]

            SOLLY

It's in the box!

Camera: back inside shoe store

                GOYSHAN
[Walking around, trying to look inconspicuous,
eating an ice cream cone with one hand, while the
other hand is carrying the box of shoes.]

                SHOE SALESMAN
  1. [Walking over to Goyshan]
May I help you?

                GOYSHAN
[Stuttering]
I would like to re…

                SHOE SALESMAN
[Rudely interrupting Goyshan]
Is that an ice cream cone in your hand?
Management specifically forbids any food or
beverages in this establishment!
[Takes Goyshan by the elbow, and leads him out of
the store.]
Please leave!

                SOLLY
[Looking at Goyshan coming out of the shoe store,
with the box of shoes still under his arm.]
What happened?

                GOYSHAN
[Child-like answer]
They don't allow ice cream in the store!

                MOLLY
They have some nerve!

                SOLLY
Hurry-up! Finish the cone!

                GOYSHAN
[Close-up on face gobbling down the ice
cream,getting the cream all over his face.]

                MOLLY

[Comes over to Goyshan, and wipes his face with a tissue.]

        GOYSHAN
[Extends his neck towards Molly to assist her.]
[Nervously.] Thank you Molly, thank you.

        SOLLY
O.K., O.K.! Now get back into the store and be assertive!

        GOYSHAN
[Under his breath] I don't like this!
[Returns to the store, with a stern look on his face.]

        SHOE SALESMAN
Now… what was it that you wanted?

        GOYSHAN
[Trying to act non-chalante]
Yes, I would like to return these shoes! [Hands the box to salesman.]

        SALESMAN
[Opens box, and starts searching for the receipt.] Do you have the sales slip?

        GOYSHAN
Err [Going into all his pockets.] [Gets very flustered.]

        SALESMAN
No receipt! No store refund! [He hands the box back to Goyshan.]

        GOYSHAN
[Turns around and leaves the store. Hands the box to Solly.]

        SOLLY
Now what?

        GOYSHAN
No receipt! No refund! [Accented with his hands spread apart, palms up.]

SOLLY

[Shoves the box back into Goyshan's hands,searching,reaches into his pockets.]Here's the sales slip! Now get back in there and demand your refund!

GOYSHAN

[Nervous] I, I really don't want to do this. There's a very mean guy in there, and I don't feel right about doing this. I feel like I'm doing something dishonest!

SOLLY

Give me the shoebox! [Grabs the box away from Goyshan!] Let me show you how it's done! [Solly charges into the store.]

Camera: Cuts to Solly being thrown out of store, with shoebox under his arm, landing on the ground.Close-up on Solly's face,stupid look,looking up.

Well, I tried!

SOLLY

Mom has an appointment with Artie, [articulates R-Tee] at the beauty parlor.[Gets back onto his feet.] Let's go!

Camera: [Follows all three through the mall to the beauty parlor entrance.] [Molly goes in, and Artie greets her with a big hug.]

SOLLY

Mom, Goyshan and I will wait for you out here, in the waiting room. I have to call Julie, to let her and Kimmy know, that I am here in Florida. I want to see Kimmy, before I return to New York.

[Goes over to wall phone and dials.] Hello, Kimmy. How are you, sweet heart? It's me!

KIMMY

[Close-up] Hi! Daddy. I miss you! Did you hear about Popu? Mommy says, Am I too young to go to the cemetery! What do you think?

                SOLLY
I think you have to listen to your mother.
Anyway, I want to see your ugly face. Is your
mother there?

                KIMMY
Hold on please…[yelling] Mom…telephone. It's
Daddy!

                JULIE
[Close-up]
[Coldly] Hello, Sol. When did you get in?

                SOLLY
This morning!

                JULIE
I suppose you want to pick Kimmy up?

                SOLLY
Can she go with Nana and me to eat Chinese? We
are at the 168th street mall, and…you are invited
too.

                JULIE
No thanks. I'm really not in the mood for
Chinese, especially Kosher Chinese. I'll bring
Kimmy to the restaurant at 6 p.m. What is the
name again?

                SOLLY
[Turns to Molly]
What's the name of that restaurant again?

                MOLLY
[Close up.] [Answers musically.]
Mosher, Kosher, Peking!

                SOLLY
[Back on telephone] Camera angle has both Molly
and Solly in view.

It's the Kosher, Mosher Peking!

                MOLLY
(Molly corrects Solly.) No Solly, it's the Mosher
Kosher, not Kosher Mosher.

[While Solly is on the telephone, we have an overlap of voices. Solly's voice is more dominant while Molly's voice is in the background.]

It has a nice musical sound to it! [Singing] Mosher, Kosher, Peking. [A little bit louder now.] Mosher, Kosher, Peking.

Camera [Molly turns and faces Goyshan.]

            GOYSHAN
Yeah, you're right! It does have a nice musical sound! He starts singing Mosher, Kosher, Peking with Molly. [Goyshan takes Molly's hands in his.]

[Molly and Goyshan are now singing together and are dancing in a small circle.]

            JULIE
What's going on there? [Annoyed] I'll see you at 6p.m. Oh, say hello to Nuna [Molly] for me.

            KIMMY
[Visual back to Kimmy] I'll see you and Nuna, at the restaurant. Thank you Daddy, I love you! I can't wait to be with you!

            SOLLY
So long. [Hangs up, turns around, and wipes his tears.] Goyshan, you are so lucky. You are going to see the most beautiful girl in the world...Kimberly Tara Batimo! My daughter! She will be meeting us for supper, at the Mosher Kosher Peking restaurant.

            GOYSHAN
Great! [Pause] You know I don't eat meat! We are vegetarians!
            MOLLY
Don't worry, Rabbi Goyshan, they serve vegetables! Their cooking is fantastic!

            SOLLY
[Whispering] Tell me, we're alone. What do you need acupuncture for?

                    GOYSHAN
Aaaa…I'm embarrassed. A…let it wait, let it wait!
[changing the subject.] How are we going to get
Molly to the cemetery?

                    SOLLY
I know. I haven't mentioned it to her yet. I'm
waiting for her to be in a good mood. Maybe,
after we finish supper.

                    GOYSHAN
[He is sitting in the waiting area, with Solly.
He then removes his yamulka, revealing a mop of
hair. He strokes his hand through it a few times,
then stands up, moves closer to the wall mirror.
Bends his head over closer. He then turns his
head to the left, then to the right, lifting his
chin up and out a couple of times.]
Maybe I'll get a slight trim.

                    MOLLY
[She is finished, and approaches the front
counter, where the cashier is standing.]

                    SOLLY
[He interdicts, and pays the cashier.]

                    GOYSHAN
Molly, you look beautiful! Do you think Artie can
give me a trim?

                    MOLLY
Oh, yes! Artie is great! [She spins around.]
Artie, darling. This is my guest Rabbi Goyshan.
Could you give him one of your special trims?

                    ARTIE
Welcome, Rabbi. Take a seat. [Swings a clean
white sheet around Goyshan, and fastens it around
his neck too tight!]

                    GOYSHAN
[Goyshan snaps his arms up to his neck, and goes
into contortions, jumping up and down from his
chair, spinning the chair around, trying to
unsnap the sheet, which is still choking him.
Gagging sounds, Deep throaty sounds. Trying to

                    45

clear his throat. He finally is successful
removing the sheet, and, completely exhausted,
slips down in the chair.]

        ARTIE
[Proceeds to use the electric hair clippers, and
chunks of hair fly off Goyshan's head.]

        GOYSHAN
[Reacts nervously to each swoop of the clippers.]
[Close-up]
Gasping, and making "oh" sounds to each swoop of
the clippers.

        ARTIE
Easy, easy big fellar!
[He puts down the clippers, and now picks up the
scissors, and clips away.]

        GOYSHAN
[Shows great relief when the clipper is put
down.] That's it! That's it! [Pointing a little
more off the side!

        SOLLY
You look wonderful Mom!

        MOLLY
[Gives Solly a big hug.] Thanks for treating me!

        GOYSHAN
[Walks over to the cashier, and pays for his hair
cut. He has a very conceited look on his face,
and continues to look at himself in the mirror
next to Solly and Molly.]

Let's go! I'm starving for that Chinese food!
Anyone have a bobby-pin?
[Gets a bobby-pin from Artie, and puts it on his
yamulka.]

[All three exit into the mall, then out the exit
into a taxi.]

Fade-out:
[Chinese Restaurant Scene]

[Taxi drops off Solly, Molly, and Goyshan in front of Mosher Kosher Peking Restaurant. All three enter, are greeted by the hostess, and are escorted to their table.]

                    WAITER
[Hands all three their menus.]

                    MOLLY
[Looking down at her menu]
Solly. Look at this wonderful menu! And everything is Kosher!

                    SOLLY
Look at this!...Phony shrimp! [Looks a little more.] Phony lobster! Phony Crab! Phony Chicken! [Talking like a wise guy.] With all this phony stuff, I think I'm going to pay the bill with Phony money!
Ha, ha, ha, [Laghing at his own joke!]

                    GOYSHAN
Laughing hysterically at Solly's joke.

                    MOLLY
Let's get the schmorgesboard!

                    SOLLY
That sounds good to me.

                    GOYSHAN
Let's do it! [Excitingly rubbing his hands together]

                    WAITER
Have you decided on your order?

                    SOLLY
We are all having the schmorgesboard!

                    WAITER

Please enjoy your meal!

[All three get up and go over to the schmorgesboard table, pick up a main dish plate, and select their favorite dishes.]

GOYSHAN

[Goyshan loads up his plate like Mt. Fuji, then returns to the table, holding his plate high over his head, spinning around, almost dropping his food like a Charlie Chaplin skit. Goyshan goes in the wrong direction, and spins out of control, out into the street, [now in fast motion] back into the restaurant, serpenting around tables, through the swinging doors, into the kitchen, back out through the swinging doors, into the dining room, then [back to normal film speed]back into his chair at the table with Solly and Molly.]

SOLLY

Let's use the chopsticks. Somehow the food tastes more Oriental. Here, Goyshan. [Hands chopsticks to Goyshan]

GOYSHAN

[Tears the paper off the wooden chop sticks. He then looks closely at Solly's hand, and tries to imitate the correct position for the sticks, but makes a mess of it, with the chopsticks shooting up into the air. He lunges after them, and lands on the floor.]

MOLLY

Rabbi Goyshan…are you alright?

GOYSHAN

[Nods his head] I'm o.k. [His head is still waving a little.][Goyshan spots the chopsticks, picks them up, then returns to his seat.]

SOLLY

Mom, please pass me the mustard.

MOLLY

Be careful, darling it's very hot!

SOLLY

I know! That's why I love it.

GOYSHAN

Please pass me the mustard, Solly, when you're

finished. [He takes a large soup spoon, and dumps a large portion on top of the pile of food on his plate. He then starts eating his food very fast.]

[Close-up on Goyshan's face, as the heat of the mustard starts to take effect. Pan back for full body shot.]

[Goyshan's hands come first to his chest. Then both hands, alternating, travel inch by inch, up to the bottom of his neck to his chin. He grabs onto his mouth, at both corners, pulling his mouth very wide open. His head is now swinging, from left to right.]

CAMERA

[Still on Goyshan]

GOYSHAN
[He is swinging his head, from left to right, like a fish trying to spit out a hook. He lets out an extra loud scream.]
hot!!

[He then springs up, and grabs the water pitcher from off the table, and guzzles it all down.]

SOLLY
[Gets up from his seat to comfort Goyshan.]
Are you all right? I told you that the mustard was hot!

CAMERA

[Pans off of Solly and Goyshan towards the entrance of restaurant, where we see Kimberly coming down the isle towards Solly, running with excitement.]

O.S. Music starts to fade in, when Kimberly appears at entrance

SOLLY
[When he sees his daughter, even though he's been away for only a short time, he turns toward her and his face lights up, and with outstretched

49

arms, goes into singing-"There's My Princess!"

Music and Singing by Solly.

CAMERA

[Unfocuses on everything, except on Kimberly.
Bright lights are added to make her stand out.

KIMMY
Daddy! Daddy!

SOLLY
[Turns around to receive his daughter's embrace.]
Kimmy, I love you so much, [hugging and kissing
her] Here, sit down between Nuna and me.

KIMMY
[Goes over to Molly and kisses her too]
Hi, Nuna.

MOLLY
Hi sweetheart. Why haven't I seen you lately?
Tell your mother I want her to call me on the
phone.

KIMMY
[Sits down, then puts her head on Solly's
shoulder.]
I knew you would be coming down, daddy, that is
for the…
[Solly grabs Kimmy, covers her mouth, thereby
keeps her from speaking.]
[Solly shushes Kimmy and gives her the sign to be
quiet by putting his finger over his lips,
without letting Molly see him.]
[Kimmy was going to say "for Popu's funeral."]
but Solly wasn't going to bring the matter up
until after Molly was finished eating.

MOLLY
[Very adamantly]
There's no secrets here! I'm not going to the
funeral tomorrow, and that's final!

SOLLY
[Changing the subject]

50

Kimmy darling, this is my friend Rabbi Goyshan.
He's on his way to Accupulco.
[Laughing wildly]

          GOYSHAN
[with a slight forced grin on his face]
[Extends his hand across the table, and
accidentally knocks over the flower vase.]
Oops, sorry. [Catches vase, and sets it back up
straight.]

          KIMMY
It's very nice to meet you Mr. Goyshan!

          MOLLY
It's not Mr. Goyshan, Kimmy, it's [with praise]
Rabbi Goyshan!

          SOLLY
What would you like to eat, Kimmy?

          KIMMY
I'll have the vegetable chow-mein. It's my
favorite!

          SOLLY
That's fine![Reaches for the bowl of vegtable
chow-mein, and hands it to Kimmy.]

          KIMMY
[Reaches out and takes some noodles, and dips
noodles into the hot mustard, then into her
mouth.]

          GOYSHAN
[Starts to warn Kimmy, but stops when he sees
that Kimmy is showing no reaction to the hot
mustard. He then looks at Solly, and gestures
with his hand with a questioned look on his
face.]

          SOLLY
Oh Kimmy has been eating this mustard since she
was very young. She's used to it!

          KIMMY

Thank you, daddy! [She starts to eat, but first puts hot mustard on top of her food.]

                GOYSHAN
[Close-up on head] Facial expression of disbelief.

                KIMMY
You know, daddy, I'm so happy you are down here in Florida. Next Monday, I've got a play. It's about Snowbirds! It would be wonderful if you could see me perform.

                SOLLY
Uh…[caught by surprise] I don't know. We'll see.

                KIMMY
It's next Monday morning, at my school at 11 am. Please come, daddy, and bring Nuna, and you are also invited Rabbi Goyshan.

                WAITER
Brings bill to Solly.

                SOLLY
Could you kindly wrap these up and make a "doggie bag" for us?

                WAITER
Thank you, no problem.

Camera Shot of everyone leaving the restaurant from rear, and camera zooms in on Solly carrying the "Doggie-bag" out the door.
[Cut to Molly's apartment.]

[Molly's Apartment]
[After Molly puts the Chinese food in the refrigerator, Solly lies down on the sofa bed, and dozes off. He still hasn't mentioned the funeral to Molly.
Goyshan is touching books on the bookshelf and removes a book, then sits down.
Molly sits next to Goyshan. She picks up knitting and proceeds to knit.]

MOLLY
Read to me Rabbi. What book did you select?

GOYSHAN
[Closes book and studies the cover.]
It's called "The Complete Siddur! It looks like a daily prayer book." [He then continues to flip the pages.]

MOLLY
Oh yes. That's the daily prayer book. Being a Rabbi, you should be very familiar with it.

GOYSHAN
[Stammering] Oh, yes! Oh! Look what I found. [Commences to read out loud.]

Man recieves his reward in the World-to-come, for the following deeds: They are:

Honoring his mother and father.
Preforming deeds of kindnness.
Early attendance in the House of Study, morning and evening.
Providing hospitality to guests.

Molly, you've earned this one for treating me so nicely.

MOLLY
[Shyly] Oh, thank you Rabbi.

GOYSHAN
[Continues to read]

Visiting the sick.
[Shakes his head up and down in agreement.]
Participating in the making of a wedding.
[Sits up straight, quickly.]
Molly, look at this one!

MOLLY
[Leans over to Goyshan's side, and peers into the book.]
What does it say?

                GOYSHAN
[Lifts his chin up, and peers at the ceiling.]
Accompanying the dead to the grave.

                MOLLY
[Reaches for the book.] Let me see that!

                GOYSHAN
[Retains the book, and points to the page.]
[Now points his finger towards Molly.]
[With emphasis.]

Accompanying the dead to the grave!

                MOLLY
[Leans backward, and sinks into the couch, drops
her head, and covers her face in shame.]

                GOYSHAN
[Continues to read, but in a very low voice.]

Concentrating on the meaning of the prayers. [In
an even lower voice.]
Making peace between a fellow man.
And the study of the Torah is equal to all the
Commandments.

Fade-out to cemetery scene.

Fade-in with pan on many people all standing
around grave site, including Molly, Solly, Kimmy,
[standing in front of her mother] Goyshan and
other family members.
All the men are wearing yarmulkas

[Pan ends on Rabbi holding a prayer book]

                RABBI
[Recites Kaddish.] (This blessing is blessing the
Lord's Name.)

"Yiskadol.......................

■■

■■

■■

[He then gives the following eulogy.]
We are taught by our Torah, to go through life
trying to accomplish the following four
commandments:
        First, we should learn to fear G-d, and
bless his name. We should always be fearful that
we are not committing sins.
        Second, we should set aside time each day to
study the Torah.
        Third, we should teach that we have learned
to our children and our children's children.
        Fourth, we should do the 613 Commandments
which we have learned from our studying of the
Torah, always keeping in mind, that when we die
our neshomers, our souls, depart from our bodies
and crossover into the next world...

    GOYSHAN
[Close up on Goyshan, nodding his head in
agreement with Rabbi, while pointing his finger
towards Solly. This gesture is to remind Solly
what he related to him on the airplane.]

    RABBI (Continues)

...And it is in the next world that we receive the
wondrous rewards for all our good deeds.
If bad things happen to us in this world, it is
because it is our punishment for the sins
committed in this world. It is G-d's way of
giving us a potch,(a slap in the behind) to try
to correct us, to get us on the right path.

    SOLLY
[Thinking]
I'd better start thinking about my neshomer,[my
soul]. My father is now in the ground...that means
I'm in the next generation to crossover, and who
knows how soon that will be? Maybe I better start
protecting my soul? Am I worthy of receiving
rewards in the next world? I haven't done any of
those commandments which the Rabbi just
mentioned. How am I going to teach Kimmy the
Torah, when she doesn't even live with me? Her

mother isn't doing anything about her Jewish
education, her Jewish tradition.

[Then everyone takes their turn in throwing some
dirt into Nat's grave.]

Camera: Rear shot of the backs of Molly, Solly-
holding Kimmy's hand, walking towards the
cemetery exit.

        KIMMY
What's the Torah, daddy?

        SOLLY
Err… [Fumbling for the right words.]
The Torah is the five books of Moses, and all the
other books together, I think!

        KIMMY
[Turning to Julie.]
You know, Mommy, you should buy me the Torah
books, so I can learn how to take care of my
soul, and learn what G-d wants me to do.
[Turning to Solly]
Daddy, do I have a soul?

        SOLLY
Sure darling, we all have souls.
[Turning towards Molly.]
You see, Mom, you did the right thing coming here
for Popu's funeral. You will get a reward for
this in the next world.
[Turns to Goyshan]
What did you tell Molly, to make her change her
mind?

        GOYSHAN
[Stuttering]
Errrr…

        SOLLY
Well, whatever you told her, it worked!
[Covering his mouth from the side]
According to your sect, we just buried a cross-

over Angel?

        GOYSHAN
[Nods his head.]
[Very low, towards Solly]
That's right! [Looks around to see if anyone had
just heard their secret]

[Close-up on just Solly and Goyshan leaving the
cemetery]

        SOLLY
[Puts his hand to his head, and removes the
yamulka.]

        GOYSHAN
Solly, why not keep the yamulka on? You would be
showing that you recognize that there is a G-d
above us all?

        SOLLY
[Puts the yamulka back on his head, reluctantly.
Here we see the inner battle that is going on
inside Solly's mind.]

Camera: [Rear, far away silhouette shot of Solly
removing the yamulka.]

        SOLLY
It's just not me!

FADE IN

Camera:. [Aerial view of Jeffery's R.V., pulling
up to a motel.]

        SANDRA
She gets out of the vehicle yelling at Jeffery.
Jeffery refuses to check into the motel because
of the cost.

        JEFFERY

Why do we always have to spend money, when we
have two perfectly good beds of our own?

57

SANDRA

Jeffery, you can sleep where you want! I'm not
going to get zebrochen! (Broken up.) I'm checking
in myself! She exits walking to motel office.
[Jeffery follows.]

MOTEL CLERK

[Handing keys to Sandra.] Two for room 611

JEFFERY

[Correcting him.] One for room 611!

MOTEL CLERK

[Close-up on clerk] Oh! I thought…

[Jeffery follows her to room]

[Inside motel room]
Sandra puts her suitcase on bed, then looks
around, picks up a towel from rack and proceeds
to dust the furniture.

JEFFERY

[Yelling] Compulsive, compulsive [angry]
compulsive cleaning disorder! You know, I never
have any pleasure with you anymore! [Angry
because he is going to be sleeping alone in R.V.]

SANDRA

Jeffery, [pause] you should know by now, whenever
you're with me, you are not going to have any
pleasure!

JEFFERY

[Inside R.V., close up on Jeffery falling asleep
behind steering wheel.]
Fade out
Fade in: [To close up of imposter state trooper,
holding a gun on Jeffery.]

STATE TROOPER

O.K. Yankee. Give me your money, and take that
Rolex off, before I blow your brains out!

JEFFERY

[Quite shaken, removes the watch, and hands it

and his money to the trooper.]

      STATE TROOPER
[He tapes Jeffery up]

Fade out:
Fade in: [To Sandra entering the R.V. in morning,
finding Jeffery taped up. As soon as she removes
the tape from Jeffery's mouth he starts screaming
at her.]

      JEFFERY
It's all your fault! If you would have been here
with me, I never would have been robbed!

      SANDRA
If I would have been here with you, I would also
have tape on my mouth! Let's call the police!

Fade out:
Fade in: [State trooper is interviewing Jeffery,
writing out the incident report.]

      STATE TROOPER
So you say that about four o'clock in the
morning, this man entered your R.V. and woke you
up, with a gun in his hand? Pointing at you? Is
that correct?

      JEFFERY
That's correct!

      STATE TROOPER
Then what happened?

      JEFFERY
He demanded that I hand over my Rolex watch,
[looks down at his empty wrist, turning his wrist
around] and my money.

      STATE TROOPER
What did he look like?

      JEFFERY
[Hesitating] Errr…

      STATE TROOPER

[Getting a little exasperated] Well, what did he look like? [Looking down at his report clipboard.]

　　　JEFFERY
[Still hesitating.] Errr… He looked, [pause] a little, [pause] like you!

　　　STATE TROOPER
[Acting a little annoyed and surprised] What do you mean …like me?

　　　JEFFERY
Not exactly like you, I mean he was a State Trooper, like you!

　　　STATE TROOPER
[Loud!] You mean to tell me you're reporting a larceny, a crime, that you say was committed by one of ours, a Georgia State Trooper?

　　　JEFFERY
[Meekly] That's right, a Georgia State Trooper!

　　　STATE TROOPER
[Turning towards Sandra] Lady…Get into your vehicle, and take this husband of yours, and get going fast, before I lock him up!

[Jeffery and Sandra quickly get into their R.V., and speed onto the highway!]

Camera: [Aerial shot of vehicle going down the highway.]

Fade out: [Voice of Jeffery, from off-screen]

　　　JEFFERY
That crook took my Rolex! I've had that watch since the Korean War! I bought it in the Navy P.X, for only $70.00! Now it will cost $1700,00 to replace! It's all your fault! If you would have agreed to fly, this never would have happened!

Camera: Fade out.

Camera: [Fade-in to Molly's living room. Pan onto
Solly who is cuddled up on the couch, while
Goyshan is sleeping on the floor on inflateable
mattress.]

[They both start to wake up from the kitchen
noise of Molly making breakfast.]

     MOLLY
[Loud] Time to wake up, boys! It's Monday
morning, and time to eat a good healthy
breakfast!

     GOYSHAN
[Close up on his head and face. His hair is a
mess, and he looks like a train had run over
him.]
[Yelling toward the kitchen] Good morning Molly!
[Turns toward Solly] Good morning Solly!
[He gets up with the blanket wrapped around him,
goes into the bathroom.]

     MOLLY
[She enters the living room, and bends down,
shakes Solly's shoulder.]
Common, Pasha,wake up. [Affectionately] I'm
making your favorite breakfast! Scrambled eggs
with Kashkaval cheese!

     SOLLY
[Pulls blanket off his head, and sits up.]
Manum. [Affectionate Greek word for Mommy]
[Solly lifts his chin smelling the delicious
aroma of the eggs and cheese.]
You're terrific!

     MOLLY
You know, every Monday we have entertainment
hour, downstairs in the auditorium. And today I
am giving a recital! So finish up, and then you
can listen to me practice.

     GOYSHAN

[Comes out of bathroom, still combing his hair and then gets dressed]
[Under his breath]That Artie is a great barber!
[Sits down at the kitchen table.]
Mmmm…smells great! What kind of eggs are these, Molly?

        SOLLY
You're in for a treat! Kashkaval, a Greek cheese melted into scrambled eggs.
Here! [Solly places a large portion into Goyshan's plate.]

        GOYSHAN
[Starts to eat.]

        SOLLY
Wait! It needs a little ketchup! He passes the ketchup bottle to Goyshan.]

        GOYSHAN
[Takes bottle, shakes it violently, then accidentally squirts to much onto his eggs.]
Oops!

        MOLLY
[Pouring coffee into the boys' cups.]
Goyshan…You are in for a treat today!
We have entertainment hour downstairs. Sam Siegel is coming! He is bringing his favorite puppet "Schmendrick"!

        SOLLY
A puppet? [In a happy surprise.]
[Solly jumps up and goes over to the telephone. He hits the buttons on the phone.]
Hello…Julie? It's me. You know there's a show here at Jewish Towers? Mom is playing the piano, and Sam Siegel is putting on a puppet show. It would be great if you could bring Kimmy!
[Pause]
The show starts at 1 P.M. Please remember to bring Kimmy! O.K.?
[Pause]
Good! Wonderful! Remember…1 P.M.!
[Solly hangs up the phone, and his mood had

changed to happy and jovial because he is going
to see Kimmy again.]

        MOLLY
[After observing the change in Solly's mood.]
Guess who's coming over to see her Nuna?
[She goes over to the piano, and sits down to
play.]
[Molly then shuffles through a large pile of
sheet music, looking for Solly's favorite pieces.
The music she selects is "Poems", by Fribisch,
Solly's favorite.]

        SOLLY
He has returned to the sofa, while Goyshan has
settled into a chair.]

[The music "Poems is a beautiful piano
composition.]

        MOLLY
[Molly starts to play the music and is distracted
by Goyshan, who compulsively picks up a fly
swatter to conduct along with Molly's playing.]

[Molly plays this piece perfectly, except when
the piece is almost finished, there is a series
of notes, which, somehow, Molly plays
incorrectly, and hits a few sour notes. She
repeats these bars a couple of times until she
plays it correctly.]

Camera: [Quick close up shots on Solly and
Goyshans' faces reaction to this disturbing
error.]

[This error, rather the lack of error becomes the
tip-off to Solly and Goyshan, later on in our
film play, that it isn't Molly who is playing,
but her cross-over angel!]

        MOLLY
[Now feeling a little more confident, she plays
Poems again perfectly, singing along with the
music.]

[Molly also sings two Greek songs, "Agape Mia"

and "Ach cananini mu micro"]

[After she finishes, both Solly and Goyshan
applaud. Goyshan wipes some tears from his eyes
because the music moved him so much.]

          GOYSHAN
That was beautiful! [Turning to Solly.] Your mom
is so talented!

          MOLLY
O.K.! O.K.! I'm ready! It's almost 12:30! Let's
get dressed and go downstairs.

Camera: Fade out

FADE IN

     JEWISH TOWERS LOBY

Fade in: [From elevator door opening, revealing
Solly, Molly, and Goyshan, exiting]

Camera: [Follows them past the main lobby
reception desk, into an auditorium with a stage,
with a piano, filled mostly with senior citizens,
with white hair.]

Friends and relatives of Jewish Towers are paying
attention to Sam, who is in the middle of a
beautiful song (Song Title "Sylvia") which he is
directing at his wife, Sylvia. She is sitting in
a wheel chair, off to the right of the stage.
[She is very pail and frail looking.] Sam's gaze
is directed at Sylvia who is just below the
stage, off to the left. Sylvia's facial
expression is one of love and adoration towards
Sam. Sam has been coming to Jewish Towers for the
last four years to entertain the sick and elderly
with music and his puppet "Schmendrick."

Sam has a flashback while he is singing to
Sylvia.

Fade to Flashback.

O.S. Background music "Sylvia" continues through entire flashback.

Sam is very young, and so is Sylvia. This scene is the remembrence of when Sam proposed to Sylvia through Schmendrick. Sam was a very shy and quiet young man. The scene opens with Sam and Sylvia sitting on a park bench. Sam is unable to come out with the words of the marriage proposal. During his vocal fumbling we hear the muffled voice of Schmendrick, coming from a suitcase next to the bench.

        SCHMENDRICK
Let me out, let me out! Sam please let me out of here!

        SAM
O.K., O.K.!
[Sam reaches over, and removes Schmendrick, and places him in between himself and Sylvia.]

        SCHMENDRICK
Sylvia, you are the most beautiful woman I ever sat next to! Can I hold your hand?

        SYLVIA
Oh yes. That would be nice!
[Sylvia picks up Schmendrick's hand and places it in hers.]

        SCHMENDRICK
If I would ask you to marry me, would you say yes?

        SYLVIA
Yes! Please ask me.

        SCHMENDRICK
Sylvia, dearest, would you let me love you forever?

        SYLVIA
Please Schmendrick...I mean Sam, please take care of me forever.

[They embrace…to fade out]

FADE IN to stage.

Camera: [Pans away from the stage area to
Auditorium entrance, where Julie and Kimmy
enter.]

        KIMMY
[She spots Goyshan, Solly, and her Nuna, and
rushes toward them. They are sitting in the front
row.] Nuna, daddy [She throws her arms around
Solly, then kisses Molly.]

        JULIE
[She bends down, and kisses Molly on the cheek,
very ceremoniously.]
Hi, Solly. Did we miss the puppet show?

        SOLLY
No! Not yet! Sit down.

        JULIE
[She sits down next to Molly, making sure she is
not next to Solly.]

        GOYSHAN
[He moves over one seat to make room for Kimmy.
Kimmy is sitting between Goyshan and Solly.]

        M.C.
And now, ladies and gentlemen, it is my privilege
to introduce Sam Siegel and his side kick,
"Schmendrick!"

        AUDIENCE
[Everyone is applauding with vigor.]

        SAM
[Sam reaches down and opens the lid, then sits
down on chair. He then bends over and removes
Schmendrick]

        AUDIENCE
[Mixed positive reactions. Laughter and smiles.
Some close ups on senior citizens' faces lighting
up.]

SCHMENDRICK

Thank you Sam for letting me breath fresh air
again! [Sarcastically] [Rub his eyes, just like
when someone awakens.] Sam, tell me. We go back a
few years since we met. How long has it been?
Forty, forty-five years?

SAM

Yes, that's about right. What's your point?

SCHMENDRICK

Well, I feel a little neglected. You're really
not taking good care of me like you'd have
everyone believe.

SAM

Why? Don't I tuck you into your box every night?
Don't I say your prayers with you?

SCHMENDRICK

Yes, that's true. But the truth is, when we first
met, your hair wasn't gray like it is
today!(Repeats) Ha, ha. Look at that, I just made
a rhyme! Your hair wasn't gray,like it is today
Anyway, your hair got gray, and mine didn't!

SAM

Ah ha……so that's what this is all about.

SCHMENDRICK

Yeah! [Pause.] I want gray hair! Look around you,
everyone here, has gray hair! Oops, I did it
again. I made a rhyme! Everyone here, has gray
hair! (Laughing to himself.)

SAM

Do you feel left out?

SCHMENDRICK

Uh huh! I think I will look more intelligent with
gray hair. More continental, smarter, more
handsome. Maybe I'll even look like a president.

SAM

Which president?

SCHMENDRICK
All the presidents! Did you ever see a picture of
a president who didn't have gray hair?

SAM
O.K.! If you insist, I'll give you gray hair!
[Sam bends over, and picks up a can of gray
paint, and a paint brush. He also wraps a towel
over Schmendrick, like in a barber shop.]

SCHMENDRICK
Do you know what you are doing?

SAM
Sure I do! Now keep still!
[Sam proceeds to paint.]
Please hold still!

SCHMENDRICK
[Yelling.] Watch out for my ears!

SAM
Please don't move!

SCHMENDRICK
[Laughing] Ha! Ha! Stop Sam, that tickles!

SAM
Are you starting to feel smarter?

SCHMENDRICK
[Humming, while Sam completes the paint job.]

SAM
[Sam accidentally paints over Schmendrick's eyes]
O.K.! Finished! How's that?

SCHMENDRICK
(Yelling) I can't see! I can't see!

SAM
You don't have to see, it came out great!
Let's ask our audience. Clap your hands if you
think Schmendrick looks great.

AUDIENCE

[Everyone claps their hands.]

Camera: Close up on Kimmy clapping very hard.

        SCHMENDRICK
[Bowing.] Thank you, thank you, thank you!
But I'd like to see for myself. Sam, please clean
off my eyes! Where's my mirror?

        SAM
[Bends over, uses a wash cloth to clean away paint
and removes a small hand held mirror from the
box, and holds it in front of Schmendrick.]
How do you like it?

        SCHMENDRICK
[Tries to see himself, but Sam keeps moving the
mirror, causing him to move, each time Sam
changes the mirror's position.]
Hold still, for crying out loud! Can't you afford
a larger mirror?

        AUDIENCE
Laughter!

        SAM
[Puts mirror back into box, and removes a larger
mirror.]
How's this.

        SCHMENDRICK
[Looking into the mirror.]
That's better! As a matter of fact, I look great!
[Looking out towards the audience.]
Don't I?

        AUDIENCE
[All applause.]

        SCHMENDRICK
Do I look like a president?

        AUDIENCE
[Mixed applause.]

        SAM

I got an idea! How would you like to look like
Napoleon?

                SCHMENDRICK
A Napoleon? Who wants to look like a piece of
pastry?

                AUDIENCE
[Strong laughter.]

                SAM
No! No! Napoleon was a great French General!

                SCHMENDRICK
O.K.! Let's try it!

                SAM
[Reaches into box and pulls out a long haired,
curly wig,that has an army hat attached,and puts
it on Schmendrick.]

                AUDIENCE
[Everyone laughing.]

                SCHMENDRICK
Let me have the mirror again!
[Looks into the mirror and jumps away.]

                SAM
What's the matter?

                SCHMENDRICK
What did you give me? You destroyed my image!
What's the sense of this? You gave me a head of
beautiful gray hair, you covered it up, and my
intelligent look is gone. You made me look like a
wooden wash mop! [Starts to cry]

                AUDIENCE
[Audience is now hysterical.]

                SAM
I'm sorry! I'm sorry! Schmendrick, come here,
I'll take it off.
[Sam tries to remove the wig, but somehow it is

stuck!]

SCHMENDRICK
What's wrong?

SAM
It's stuck!

SCHMENDRICK
You dummy! [Quickly covers mouth with his hand.]
Oops! Why didn't you wait for the gray paint to
dry? Now I have to spend the rest of my life
looking like a French fagila! (Homosexual)

AUDIENCE
Wild laughter

SAM
[Still trying to remove the wig.]
I think it's coming off!

SCHMENDRICK
I surely hope so!

SAM
[Pulls wig completely off.]

SCHMENDRICK
Wow! That's a relief!

SAM
[To audience.]
Doesn't Schmendrick look better now?

AUDIENCE
[Everyone yells together.] Yeah!

SAM
[Concludes his act, Schmendrick waves goodbye,
and is placed back into his box. Sam stands up
and bows to the audience.]

AUDIENCE
[Heavy applause.]

SAM
And now, I know you have all been waiting for
her, it is my pleasure to give you, your very
own…Molly Batimo! [Sam escorts Molly to the
piano, and then leaves the stage and sits down
next to his wife Sylvia [in wheelchair].]

MOLLY
[Molly plays, and sings favorite Jewish songs.
She also plays "Poems." Again, when she gets to
the same difficult part, she errors, but corrects
very fast, then continues.]

KIMMY
[Close up.]
[Kimmy applauds very energetically after each
song. She is now sitting on Solly's lap.]

SOLLY
[Holds Kimmy's hands, claps together with her.
When Molly plays, a fast Greek melody, Solly
jumps out of his seat, grabs Kimmy, starts
dancing, then pulls Goyshan off his seat, and
continues to dance in circles with Kimmy and
Goyshan.]

AUDIENCE
[Then the other tenants from the building stand
up and form little groups of dancers, forming
circles. The whole auditorium is full of joy and
smiles.]

SOLLY
[He tries to pull Julie off her chair to dance,
but she refuses.]

CLARINET PLAYER
[Close up on him, standing next to piano.] Solo.

MOLLY
[Molly's last song is "Hatikva"]
AUDIENCE
[Everyone is singing and swaying!]
[When this song ends, everyone returns to their
seats.]

                M.C.
Thank you Molly! Let's all of us give a big hand
to our very own… Molly Batimo!

                Molly
[Molly takes a few bows, then returns to her
seat, escorted by Solly.]

                M.C.
And now, to finish off our wonderful show, we are
bringing back, Sam Siegle to play for you, and
Sylvia, his recently completed ballad,
"Snowbird".

                SAM
[Sam stands up, bends down, and kisses Sylvia,
before he walks up onto the stage then over to
the piano.]

                AUDIENCE
[The whole room goes quiet, as Sam starts
playing.]

                SAM
"SNOWBIRD"

You're my precious Snowbird,
You're my loving Snowbird.

Together we leave before the first snow,
through clouds and rainbows, we joyed to know.

You're my beautiful Snowbird,
you're loving Snowbird.

Ahead, ahead waiting,
for another new spring.

You're my sharing Snowbird,
you're my caring Snowbird.

You turn a long journey,
into a timeless glide.

The long trip becomes short,
with you by my side.

You're my precious Snowbird,
you're my loving friend,

And at the end…
should I fly away before thee,
know for certain,
I'll be waiting for you, impatiently.

        AUDIENCE
[Everyone had tears in their eyes from Sam's
beautiful ballad directed toward Sylvia.]

        M.C.
That's our show friends. Let's all give a show of
appreciation to Sam, Molly, and everyone who made
this afternoon so joyful and happy!

        AUDIENCE
[Applause!]

        MOLLY
[Everyone, Solly, Kimmy, and Goyshan, go over to
Molly and give her a hug of appreciation.]

        SOLLY
I've got a great idea! Let's all go for some ice
cream!

        KIMMY
That's great! Can we go, Mommy?

        JULIE
No, I don't think so. We have to get going.
Tomorrow is school. We have to get home.

        KIMMY
That's not fair! I want to spend more time with
Nuna and daddy.

        JULIE
[Coldly] We'll visit again, when your father
decides to see you.

        KIMMY

[Holding onto Solly.] Please mommy, [crying] please…

          JULIE
[Pulls Kimmy away, and leaves the auditorium.]

          SOLLY
[Heartbroken, all choked up. Turns to Molly.]
Manum…You were terrific!

          MOLLY
[Close up]
Come, Pasha, everything is for the good.

[People surrounding Molly, some giving pats on the shoulder.]

          FRIEND
You were wonderful, Molly!

          SOLLY
[Walks out of the auditorium to entrance door, and looks out on avenue in the direction where Kimmy went.]

Fade out: on Goyshan walking over to Solly, and puts his arm around him, with tears in his eyes.

Fade in: [Back in Molly's apartment.]

          SOLLY
Come on, Manum, let's have a little Greek music to cheer us up!

          GOYSHAN
[Picks up butter knife in anticipation, to use as his baton.]

          MOLLY
[She sits down at the piano, and begins to play. After one piece, she turns around to Solly.]
You have to help me, Chuch-a-colu. [This implies to Solly, that he should take out his mandolin from the closet and accompany Molly.]

          SOLLY

O.K.!
[Solly goes over to the closet and removes his mandolin, then sits down next to Molly.]

        SOLLY & MOLLY
[They play a beautiful duet called "Agapi Me" and also sing.]

        GOYSHAN
[He applouds when they finish.]

        SOLLY & MOLLY
[Now they play a lively classical Greek dance piece.]

        GOYSHAN
[He's really into this music. He throws his hands above his head, true Greek style, and dances around the living room. Goyshan takes out a handkerchief, and Solly grabs hold, now dancing together around the apartment. When they enter the kitchen Solly opens the refrigerator.]

        SOLLY
Who's hungry? [Bends knees, to get a better look.]
What an idea!
[Solly picks up his mandolin and a pencil. Takes a piece of paper, and starts writing down the words to the following song: Out loud he proclaims] "SECOND HAND CHOWMEIN!"

        GOYSHAN
That's a great idea!

        MOLLY
I love it!

        SOLLY

"SECOND HAND CHOWMEIN"

Did you ever wake up,
in the middle of the night?

From a bad dream,

startled with fright?

Your thinking taste buds,
give you a great idea!

Maybe a little snack,
there they are, hiding in the back.

Cute, adorable, little white boxes,
So tempting so opportunity knocks.

There is nothing like it,
Maybe a little toxic,

It's hard to explain,
there's no taste like it,
Second hand chow mein!

Hiding in their doggie bags,
Cute adorable, little white boxes,

But I'm on their trail,
like seven hungry foxes.

Comon out little doggies,
comon out little doggies,
you can wag your tails,
in the micro-wave oven,

And when the bell rings, my stomach sings...
there is nothing so delicious as second hand
chowmein!

Second hand chow mein
second hand chow mein,

The thought of it,
Preys on my brain.

Tasting it does the same.

Second hand chowmein,
second hand chowmein,

Eating it,
drives me insane.

There's nothing like it, sheh, sheh,
second hand chow mein,

Second hand, sheh, sheh,
second hand, sheh, sheh,

Second hand chowmein.

What? No fortune cookie?

[After Solly finishes the song, Molly and Goyshan applause.]

GOYSHAN
That was great, Solly...I didn't realize you were so talented.

MOLLY

You have just given me a mother's nachas!
[Pleasure.]

[Phone rings] [Molly picks it up, and it is Kimmy.]

KIMMY
Hello...Nuna! It's me! How are you? I just loved your performance! You were so cool! Is daddy there?

MOLLY
[Hands phone to Solly.]
It's for you, Solly. Our wonderful princess misses her daddy!

SOLLY
Hello darling. Are you O.K.? Wasn't Schmendrick great?

KIMMY
Oh, he was great. Thank you for inviting me to see him. That's why I'm calling you. You see, there is another performance coming up! Next Sunday! And you have to see it!

            SOLLY

Really! But I was going to return to White Lake
next Sunday!

      KIMMY
You have to put it off!

      SOLLY
But why should I put it off?

      KIMMY
Because, on Sunday, I forgot to tell you. My
school is putting on a very important play, and I
am in it! And I want you to see me. Please daddy!

      SOLLY
Kimmy, I wouldn't miss your performance, for
anything, darling! You can count on Nuna and
Goyshan and me to be there!

      KIMMY
Thank you daddy! I love you so much!

Fade out:

Fade in: [Backstage in school. Teachers and
parents are preparing their little actors and
actresses for the play.]

[Kimmy is all dressed up in a beautiful white
bird costume. There are also other little girls
dressed up in bird costumes, however, Kimmy has
the only white one.
They are all behind the main stage curtain.]

Cut to: [Front view of curtain.]
Lighting: [Lights dim. Spotlight on Teacher M.C.]

      TEACHER MC
[Comes out to center stage.]
Welcome! Welcome! Welcome everyone!

Camera: [Scans audience, and comes to stop on
front row, where Solly, Goyshan, Molly and Julie
are seated.]

                        79

TEACHER MC
Welcome parents, welcome friends and students of
P.S. 159. Today we are presenting to you a short,
delightful play called "Snowbirds."

Music: [Coming from behind curtain.]

Camera: [Cut to : Short take of teacher
controlling the record player backstage.]
[Now, back to teacher with mike, front stage.]

TEACHER MGR
The purpose of our play, is to teach our children
how to better inter-react with our seniors, who
come from all over the United States and Canada,
into our neighborhoods. Then, when the northern
winter is over, they return to their summer
homes.
We are fortunate and lucky to have them here! We
meet them daily in our lives. In the
supermarkets, in the shopping malls, in our parks
and beaches. We want our young ones to learn to
be more sensitive and caring, and to react more
positively to the many rewarding associations
with our Snowbirds.
And now, let our play begin.
[Leaves stage.]

Lighting: [Spotlight off.]

Camera: [Pulls back to capture entire stage.]

Stage: [The curtains open. Ten little actors and
actresses are flapping their wings, going around
in a circle, to the tempo of the music "Hawaiian
Wedding Song."]

AUDIENCE
[Applause.]

Camera: [Close up on front row, where our family
is sitting.]

                    SOLLY
Which bird is Kimmy?
[Stands up in front row.]

                    PARENT
[Sitting in back of Solly.]
Please sit down, Sir, we can't see through you!

                    SOLLY
[Solly sits down.]
Oh yes. Now I see her. See Mom, [pointing] on the
far left side of the stage.

                    MOLLY
[Excited.]
I see her! I see her!

Stage: [The circling of birds stops, and a single
bird breaks off formation, and moves around the
perimeter, flapping his wings, coming to a stop
in front center stage, in front of a standing
microphone.]

                    1st BIRD
[Bright yellow feathers. Boy in costume.]
Hi, everyone! I'm snowbird! Boy, am I tired! I
just flew down from Detroit, Michigan. That's my
summer home. We manufacture cars for the whole
world in my city. The winters are severe. I love
to live here in Florida! There is so much water
down here. I have a choice of eating salty fish
from the ocean, or sweet fish from the lakes,
even though the alligators are a little scary.
[Starts flapping his wings, turns around waves
goodbye.]
Bye!
[Flaps back to his original spot in circle.]

                    AUDIENCE
[Applause.]

                    2nd BIRD
[Bright blue feathers. Repeats movement procedure
of 1st bird , and comes to a stop in front of
microphone.]

[Girl Bird.]
Hi, everyone! Wow! That was some trip. I flew down from my home in Boston, Mass. Boston has so many wonderful colleges and universities! It is also the center for electronic research. Our baseball team, the Boston Red Socks, won the World Series! Cape Cod, has beautiful boating and beautiful beaches, just like Florida. Bye!
[Starts flapping her wings, and flies back to her spot in circle.]

        AUDIENCE
[Applause.]

[During the entire play, parents are setting off flashbulbs from their cameras.]

        3rd BIRD
[Girl in bright red feathers, stops in front of mike.]
Hi, everyone! I'm a cardinal. I just flew down from Toledo, Ohio. Boy! Does it get cold in Toledo. The northwest winds blow so strong..and the snow...piled up to four feet! Do you know what Toledo, Ohio is famous for? Let's see,...First scales.Next time you step on a scale, I bet it says made in Toledo. Second, they manufacture glass windshields for all the automobiles. Third,they grow a lot of tomatoes all around Toledo, because the soil there is very rich and fertile. The farmers harvest thousands of bushels, and guess what favorite food they make?
[Pulls out a ketchup bottle] That's right...KETCHUP!

        AUDIENCE
Laughter!

        3rd BIRD
I love to come to Florida because it is so nice and warm. So...remember, whenever you eat French fries and hamburgers,...think of my home town, Toledo, Ohio! Bye!
[Starts flapping, and returns to her spot in circle.]

        AUDIENCE

Applause.

        4th BIRD
[Kimmy. Dressed-up as a bird in a completely
white costume. She flaps her wings,then flys
around the perimeter of circle, then stops in the
center in front of the microphone.]

        KIMMY
Hi, everyone. Guess where I just flew down from?
White Lake, New York! What? You never heard of
White Lake, N.Y.? Well, I'm sure you heard of the
Catskill Mountains,Grossingers,the Concord Hotel.
Most important, that's where my daddy is from!
[Kimmy steps forward to the edge of the stage,
and talks directly to Solly.] Stand up,daddy!
He's such a wonderful Snowbird. He flies down
here, not once a year, like everyone else, but
sometimes,six times a year! Whenever my Nuna
needs him. Stand up,daddy,..he's a SUPER
Snowbird! Stand up Nuna!

[They both stand up, and the audience applaudes.]

        AUDIENCE
Laughter!

        SOLLY
[He stands up, gives a little wave, then sits
down.]

        KIMMY
[She backs up to her original position behind the
microphone.]

White Lake has great fishing, and delicious
blueberries! It even has a summer kosher grocery
stor.
[We hear Kimmy's inner voice. "I wish I lived in
White Lake".]
I have to fly off right now, because I have a
friend waiting at Parrot Jungle.

            AUDIENCE
Applause.

            KIMMY
[Turns around and returns to her spot in the
circle.]

            SOLLY
[Applauding very loud. He has a proud look on his
face for his daughter's beautiful performance.]

[Far shot]

[All of our Snowbirds start flapping, and revolve
in a circle, as the curtain comes down.]

            AUDIENCE
Applause.

            TEACHER MC
[She comes out to center stage.]
Weren't they great? [Applauding for students.]

            AUDIENCE
Applause.

            TEACHER MC
I have a message,[reading from paper] from one of
my dearest friends, Emily, a snowbird too! She
wants me to convey her precious thoughts to our
young snowbirds.
Most of us snowbirds have passed the sixtieth
year mark, and have become more concerned with
the world to come. We hope the world to come,
doesn't come for another sixty years!

            AUDIENCE
Laughter.

            TEACHER MC

[Continues to read.]
But if we cross over before then, we will be

bringing our good deeds with us. We will also be bringing the records of our bad deed. One bad deed, which I would like to refer to, which our young snowbirds may not be aware of, is hurting people's feelings with words. Words can hurt very deeply. Therefore, as you are growing up, try to remember to be very careful not to hurt another persons' feelings, with words. Once the words are out of your mouth, you cannot take them back!

Thank you Emily, for this beautiful recommendation.

Let's all give a round of applause for all of our talented snowbirds.

        AUDIENCE
Applause! [Standing up.]

        FADE OUT

        FADE IN
[Camera shooting through windshield of Jeffrey's R.V.] Jeffry and Sandra are still on the highway, sitting in bumper to bumper traffic, filled with snowbirds heading south.

        JEFFREY
[Yelling at Sandra, then yelling out the window.] You stupid snowbirds! Get the lead out of your pants! Do you think you are going to live forever?

[There is a car to the left of Jeffrey, a women driver, wearing a helmut. There is a prominent logo on the back of her helmut showing the letters O.L.D. Inc.. She is speaking into her C.B. microphone, and communicating with other women drivers who are wearing the same helmuts. They belong to a group of Snowbirds who transport cars to and from Florida, and who work for a company called O.L.D.Inc.,Overland, Long, Distance.)

        WOMEN DRIVER

[Into mike] O.K. girls, we got a loud mouthed
R.V. to my right. Let's quiet him down!

[Aerial shot of four cars maneuvering and finally
boxing in Jeffrey! They all get out of their cars
and walk over to Jeffry.They are going to give
him a piece of their minds.]
        JEFFREY
[Pointing to the traffic.] Did you ever see such
a mess of Snowbirds?
        FOUR LADY DRIVERS
[They take off their helmuts simultaneously,
revealing that they are Snowbirds too!]

        FADE OUT

        FADE IN
[Solly and Goyshan are boarding their plane back
to New York, and are coming down the isle. They
take their seats. After they get settled,Goyshan
looks to his left, then makes a double take!
Sitting to his left, in the same seat as their
trip down, is Yenta!.]

        YENTA
Hi!.You look very familiar. Are you a Snowbird?
Are you Jewish?

        GOYSHAN
[Turns to Solly, and points to Yenta.]

        SOLLY
Oh no!

[Outside shot of jet taking off.]

        SOLLY
[Puts on headphones, and we hear the music
"Poems"]

        FADE OUT

[On Solly and Goyshan, closing their eyes and
dozing off.]

FADE IN

[Exterior Solly's house. Goyshan and Solly are
raking leaves.]

(Background sad Jewish music on violin.)

        SOLLY
[Solly is very sad.]

        GOYSHAN
[He is raking leaves, and each time he looks up,
his face reflects Solly's sadness.
In order to try to change Solly's down mood, he
starts humming a happy tune which he heard Molly
playing. He picks up the speed of his raking in
time to the music he is humming. As the music
picks up tempo, Solly changes his hand position
on the rake, as if he was dancing with a real
partner.]

Come on Solly. Snap Out of it! Come…dance with
me.

        SOLLY
[Pushes him away, but then gives in, and starts
dancing with Goyshan.]
(He also starts humming the music, louder than
Goyshan.)

        RABBI FISHBONE
Solly, it's so wonderful to see you and your
friend getting into the holiday spirit, with Rosh
Hashonah just around the corner. Can we count on
you and your friend for our Minyon? You know,
with all the Snowbirds gone south, it is very
difficult to have ten men in Schull for our
prayer sessions?

        SOLLY
I don't know, Rabbi,(O.S. How do I get out of
this?) Let me think about it. I'll let you know.

        RABBI FISHBONE

[He takes Solly aside, away from Goyshan.]
(Softly) Solly, we are having a little financial
problem at our Schull. We need to fix-up, and
paint the Synagogue for the on coming holidays...If
there is a chance for you to make a small
contribution, it would be greatly appreciated.

        SOLLY
How much money are you short?

        RABBI FISHBONE
(Hesitantly)...A little under ten thousand dollars!

        SOLLY
Wow! I'll drop off a small check later on this
week.

O.S.(Sympathetically to himself)
The Rabbi sure has a money problem. I wish I
could help more!

        RABBI FISHBONE
Thank you Solly...Zeigesundt!

        GOYSHAN
(Covering his mouth, to Solly.) What does that
mean...(Messing up the Yiddish pronunciation.)
Zei ge brundt?

        SOLLY
It means "have good health!"

        GOYSHAN
[Quickly turning to Rabbi Fishbone.]
(Blurting out) And good health to you, Rabbi!

        SOLLY
I'm sorry, Rabbi. I haven't introduced you to my
guest. This is..(Starts to say Rabbi, then cuts
himself short.)...Mr.Goyshan.

        RABBI FISHBONE
[Extends his hand to Goyshan, and shakes his
hand.] It is my pleasure to meet you. Welcome to
White Lake! [Looking at Goyshan's yalmulkah.]
Where do you daven?

GOYSHAN
[Turns to Solly with a questioned look on his
face.]
What's that?

SOLLY
He means, where do you pray?

GOYSHAN
(Nervously) Er, er, er,…

RABBI FISHBONE
[Realizing that he is embarassing Goyshan, he
changes the subject.]
That's nice, and don't forget to prepare for
Succoth! If you need any help building your
Succah, please feel free to call on me for help.
You know, there is a wonderful Succah factory in
South Fallsburg, where you can get everything to
build your Succah, including your Luluv.
[He then departs.]

GOYSHAN
What's a Succah?

SOLLY
[Thinking.] Oh, yes! A Succoth is a temporary
shed, which we are commanded to build every
holiday season, to remember how Moses and the
Jewish nation lived for forty years in the
desert, when they left Egypt. We are commanded to
spend as much time, in the Succoth, as possible

GOYSHAN
Does that mean, if we have a Succoth, we can eat
and sleep in it?

SOLLY
That's correct!

GOYSHAN
Sounds like fun!
Solly, what does "Rabbi" mean? You called me
"Rabbi" to your mother, when we down in Florida.

89

SOLLY
It means "Teacher"!

GOYSHAN
How am I a teacher? What did I teach you?

SOLLY
[Thinking first]
Don't you remember, on the plane down to Florida?
You told me all about that silly story of the
(hesitates) Cross-Over Angels?

GOYSHAN

[Looking up at the sky.]
Oh year. That's right!

FADE-OUT

FADE-IN
[Interior]
[Solly's kitchen. Solly and Goyshan are sitting at
kitchen table.]

SOLLY
[Solly gets up, and goes over to refrigerator.]
Goyshan...You've got to taste this pickled herring!
It's out of this world! [Solly tries to open the
jar, but it is stuck. He tries again, but he can't
open it.]
Here... [He hands the jar to Goyshan.] You try it.

GOYSHAN
[Takes jar and tries to open it, but it won't
open.]
(Grunting)
[He continues struggling. He stands up, and goes
through contusions trying to open the jar. It
finally opens, leaving Goyshan wiped-out. He
carefully hands the jar to Solly to serve the
pickled herring.]

SOLLY

[He serves the fish, then digs in with Goyshan.]
Well. How do you like it? It's great herring,
isn't it?[He is waiting for positive response
from Goyshan, but he is too busy stuffing his
mouth with fish that he can't talk.]

        GOYSHAN
[After finishing, he sits back, content, with
both his hands on his stomach.After resting a few
minutes, he reacts violently to a great pain in
his left, big toe.
(Loud.)Yikes! Ow! Oh! There it goes again!
[Jumps up from chair, grabs left foot, then
starts hopping around the kitchen.]
Now you know why I need acupuncture. Someone told
me that I could cure my gout with acupuncture!

        SOLLY
Okay, okay! Let's go! Hop out to the car, while
I call Dr.Chan.
[Solly goes over to the phone, while Goyshan hops
out of kitchen towards door.]

        FADE OUT

        FADE IN
[Exterior of Dr.Chan's house.]
[Close up on big sign on lawn."ACUPUNCTURE"
From sign we pan on backs of Goyshan and Solly
entering house.

        CUT TO
[Interior. Solly and Goyshan enter office, and
sit down in waiting room.]

        RECEPTIONIST (Oriental women.)
[Holding clip board, she approaches Goyshan.]
Dr. Chan will see you now. Come right this way.

        SOLLY and GOYSHAN
[Both get up, and Solly lets Goyshan lean on him,
like a crutch, and they hop their way into Dr.
Chan's examining room.]

Close up on Goyshan's face, showing his pain and
suffering.
Then camera pans over to Dr.Chan, who is standing
on far side of the room, with his back to us.]

        DR.CHAN
(Strong Jewish accent.)
Vait a minute. I'll be right with you!

[Zoom in on Dr. Chan, as he spins around,
revealing he is not a Chinese doctor, but a
Jewish Doctor,even brandishing a full beard!]

Please lie down on the table, boychick!

        GOYSHAN
[Hops over to examining table.]

        DR.CHAN
(Talking to Solly.) Please take off his shoe.

        SOLLY
[As he is taking off Goyshan's shoe.] You don't
look Chinese!

        DR.CHAN
Who says I have to look Chinese? Who were you
expecting...Jackie Chan? Will your friend feel
better if I look Chinese?

        SOLLY
[Dumbfounded look on his face.]
We thought, with your name being "Chan", you
were...

        DR.CHAN
(Interrupts Solly)
Yes! Yes!...My name was originally "Chanowitz",
when my father came here from Russia.
So vie cut it down to "Chan".Is that a crime?
[Continues to examine Goyshan's foot.]
Vat makes you think that vie Jews don't know how
to give the needle? Ha, ha, ha. That's my
favorite funny!
(Talking to Goyshan.) My boychick, you have a
very bad case of the gout! Acupuncture cannot
cure gout! You have to stop eating salty, spicy

foods! Take these pills with food, three times a
day, and you will be back to normal!

          FADE OUT

O.S. (Dr. Chan's voice) …and stay away from
pickled herring!

          FADE IN
[Solly's bedroom.]

          SOLLY
[Solly is in bed, all tucked in, and we zoom in
on him as he falls asleep.]

          FADE OUT

          FADE IN
[Rabbi's library room, White Lake Synagogue.]
This room is filled with, ceiling to floor
shelves of old and new books of Torah. In the
center of the room is a large conference table
with ten chairs. Rabbi Fishbone is seated at the
head. There are seven other Rabbis, plus Solly
and Goyshan.]
[Our scene opens with what appears to be an
unsolvable dilemma. Everyone is screaming at each
other.Apparently the board of directors have
reached a crisis.]

          RABBI FISHBONE
[Slams the table with his wooden gavel.]
Gentlemen! Gentlemen! Let's have a little order
here! So far, we have come to the conclusion that
we cannot put off painting the outside of our
Schull again,for another year. The holidays will
be upon us in approximately sixth days, leaving
us very little time to raise the ten thousand
dollars needed.Rabbi Cohen, our Treasurer, has
informed me that we have …exactly…[picks up

paper] five hundred and forty five dollars. What
can we do to raise the rest? Who has a good idea?

    RABBI SHAPIRO
[Stands up] How about a raffle? [Looks around
table for approval.]

    EVERYONE
No! No! No!
[Rabbi Shapiro sits down with disappointed look.]

    RABBI FELDMAN
[Stands up, with enthusiasm] How about a SUPER
Bingo? [Looks around table for support.]

    EVERYONE
No! No! No!

    RABBI COHEN
[Jumps up!] I've got it! I've got it! Lets make a
Chinese Auction!

    RABBI SHAPIRO
What's a Chinese Auction? [Pointing a scolding
finger at Rabbi Cohen.] Don't you know that
slavery is illegal! And who would want to own a
Chinick anyway?

    RABBI GROSS [He is a Little Person.]
That's not a bad idea! And not expensive! How
much could rice cost for a year?

    EVERYONE
No! No! No! (All resume yelling again at each
other.)

    RABBI FISHBONE
[Hits the table again.] Order! Order!Order! Can't
Any of you Talmud Chocums(Wise person.)come up
with a good idea?

    SOLLY
[He raises his hand, but no one pays attention to
him.]

RABBI SHAPIRO
(Shushes Solly.)

EVERYONE
(They all start fighting again.)

SOLLY
[Raises his hand, stands up, and trys to be
heard.]
I have a great idea!

RABBI FISHBONE
(Loud.) Quiet, everyone! Our good friend and
neighbor Solly Batimo has an idea. Please give
him the courtesy to be heard. [Turns to Solly.]
Go ahead, Solly! Let's hear your idea.

SOLLY
[The whole room goes silent. All heads turn
toward Solly. Everyone leans forward.]

SOLLY
[Solly hesitates. He feels the pressure of
everyone's eyes upon him]

RABBI GROSS
[His little hands outstretched] Nu? (Well?)

SOLLY
You've all heard of the PLO?... Let's have a WLO!
What does WLO stand for?

RABBI FISHBONE
(Guessing) Something to do with the Arabs?

SOLLY
[Solly moves his head from left to right.]
No!

EVERYONE
[All looking at each other, with shrugging
shoulders and outstretched palms]

(In unison) Vot's W.L.O.?

        SOLLY
(After a brief silence.)
WLO stands for White Lake Olympics! Why don't we
have an Olympics?

        EVERYONE
[They are all speechless. The whole room goes
silent. Everyone is stunned and perplexed by
Solly's idea.. Everyone is looking at each other.
This idea has come to them from a different
realm. They all look at Rabbi Fishbone for his
reaction. Maybe he knows what Solly is talking
about.]

        RABBI FISHBONE
[Zoom in]
[Lifts his right hand to his chin, cocks his head
to the left, stands up,walks around, in a tight
circle, then sits down and then directs his gaze
at Solly.]
Could you please explain to us, Solly...how we can
have (loud) an Olympics, here in White Lake? We
are not living in Sydney Australia, or Beijing
China, or Athens Greece with gigantic stadiums
and swimming pools.

        SOLLY
[Sees he has the groups attention, stands erect,
with a lot of courage.]
Let's call it, a Baby Olympics. Maybe a water
games decatheron, or whatever they call it when
there is a series of athletic events. Let's look
at our assets.

        EVERYONE
[They all look at each other, questionally.]

        RABBI COHEN
Assets? Vat assets?

        RABBI KLEIN
I think he's gone Mashugger! (Crazy.)

                96

RABBI FISHBONE
Wait! Wait! Let's hear him out!

SOLLY
(Continues to express his idea.)
Our biggest asset is what G-d has given us. Our
beautiful lake! [Gesturing with his hand toward
the window.]

RABBI COHEN
What do you expect us to do? Make the lake part
in the middle? Moses doesn't own a home on the
lake.[Looks around.] Does he?

RABBI HALBERSHMEAR
Maybe Solly means we should bottle the water, and
sell it?

RABBI FISHBONE
Solly. Please explain how we are going to have a
baby Olympics, and raise money from it.

SOLLY
Very …(drags word out)simple! We have a great
race, on the water. This race is made up of
different competitions. The first part of the
race could be a swimming race. The second part
could be a jet-ski race. The third part could be
a water-skiing race ending with a running
race.Yes, [nodding] ending with a mad dash to the
finish line.

RABBI FISHBONE
[He is now caught up with Solly's enthusiasm.]
Yes! Yes! But how do we make money?

SOLLY
I'd thought you'd never ask! Very simple. [Solly
walks triumphantly around the whole table, and
then up to Rabbi Fishbone.]
Everyone coming to our Whit Lake Olympics, first
must pay an admission fee to get in.

EVERYONE
Ah, hah…(Draging out the hah.)

            SOLLY
Then we have food stands, with hot dogs, French
fries, knishes, pizza, pop   corn, and plenty of
cold drinks.

            RABBI GROSS
Can we have frozen custard?

            SOLLY
Definitely!

            RABBI UNGAR
But that's still _not_ ten thousand dollars!

            SOLLY
[Starts to wealk aound the table again, now in
the opposite direction. Everyone has their eyes
fixed on Solly, watching him attentively.]
Why shoot for only ten thousand? Maybe, with my
final idea, we can take in twenty thousand, or
maybe even thirty thousand dollars!

            RABBI FISHBONE
Oh, oh! Something is starting to sound fishy!
Solly, this idea better be kosher!

            RABBI KAMINSKY
[Interupts Rabbi Fishbone's direction of
thought.] Vill this Olympics be a religious ,
non-profit event? There could be tax problems.

            RABBI FISHBONE
[Close-up, directing his attention to Solly.] So…
(Dragged out.]

            SOLLY
Yes! Yes! Rabbi. The whole Olympics will be
KOSHER! Don't worry!
[Solly puts his hand to his chin, in a thinking
mood.] We will put flags up, all around the lake,
and up and down Route 17B…

            RABBI FISHBONE
(Interupts Solly) Stop! With the flags! How do
we raise money from the races, without breaking
the law?

SOLLY

We have ten contestants. Each one has a number on
their chest and back,
From one to ten. Each person picks the number who
they think is going to win. Then we set up
betting windows, like at the track. Let's call
them "Donation Windows!" A one dollar window, a
five dollar window, a ten dollar window, a twenty
dollar window, a fifty dollar window, and
(excitingly).. a one hundred dollar window! Then,
when the race is over, we pay the lucky winning
ticket holders twice the amount they donated.
The beautiful thing here is, there are ten
numbers, and we only pay out the money on one
number. All the money taken in on the losing nine
numbers goes to us! Get it?

RABBI HALBERSHMEAR

Does anyone win for second and third?

SOLLY

Maybe we will pay for second and third, but that
gentlemen, is up to you. If we do, we will be
paying out more, and lose money , leaving less
money for renovations.

RABBI HALBERSHMEAR

Vie better not! We don't vant to lose money!

RABBI FISHBONE

It sounds like we should take a vote on Solly's
brilliant idea. Everyone in favor...say Ai!

EVERYONE

(Loud) Ai!   [Everyone has raised their hands.]

RABBI FISHBONE

Anyone opposed, say "NAY"!   [No hands are raised.]
Passed! I guess it is unanimous!

EVERYONE

[Everyone is standing and shaking hands with each
other.]

GOYSHAN

[Goes over to Solly and shakes his hand.]
Solly, you were just great!

        SOLLY
[Close-up.]
[Solly is enjoying his new found notoriety, which
is written all over his face.]
Okay, gentlemen, please sit down!

[Solly reaches over to Rabbi Fishbone's loose
leaf book, and removes ten sheets of paper.]

        EVERYONE
[Everyone is watching Solly closely. They all
have a puzzled look on their faces.]

        RABBI KAPLAN
Vot's he doing?

        SOLLY
[Solly is writing a large number on each piece of
paper. When he is finished, he shuffles the
papers, and places the pile, face down on the
table.]
This is it, gentlemen. You just voted yourselves
in, as contestants in the White Lake Olympics!

        EVERYONE
[Suddenly they all realize that they will be the
ten contestants. There are obvious facial
expressions, under-the- breath comments, as the
reality sinks in.

        SOLLY
[Observing their nervousness, Solly distracts
them, before they start backing out.]
O.K. gentlemen! It's time for us to pick our
numbers.

        EVERYONE
[They all stand up, and form a line in front of
Solly. Then, one by one, they pick the top sheet
of paper, revealing their numbers.]

            GOYSHAN
[After he picks his number, he exclaims his
delight!]
My lucky number...seven!

            RABBI GROSS
Being a Little Person, he has to climb up on the
chair, but before he can take his number, Rabbi
Kaplan pulls him away.]
Let me go! [Struggling.] Let me go! Put me down!

            RABBI KAPLAN
You're too small to be a contestant!

RABBI GROSS
I'm too small to do what? Are you afraid I might
beat you?
[He climbs up the chair again, and snatches the
paper,looks at it, then presses it against his
chest, exclaiming with happiness...]
Wow! I'm number one!

            SOLLY
[Picks up the last sheet of paper with the number
ten on it.]

    `  `

    FADE OUT.

INGREDIENTS FOR W.L.O. [White Lake Olympics]

1. Total area roped off for spectators.

2. Special area roped off for Contestants.

3. On Lake shore, special area roped off for boats.

4. Lake sectioned off with buoys, floating marker flags and rafts.

5. Life saving towers, with first aid stations.

6. Tent award area for announcers, MC's, and bands.

7. Large area roped off for food concessions. One area marked "MILK", and the other area marked "MEAT".

8. Multiple kiosks with photographs of each Rabbi wearing their numbers pasted up onto each "donation window"

9. Security Police area.

10. Media, T.V. crew area.

11. Olympic Torch Lighting area.

12. Judges stand.

13. Track area with "Finish Line".

14. Fire truck area.

15. EMS vehicle area.

16. State Trooper and Sherriff area.

17. Rest-room area.

[During the filming of the W.L.O. competitions, we will create maximum action stunts to afford excitement, thrills, suspense and laughter.

This is maximized before our eyes due to the fact that our contestants are out-of-shape middle aged Rabbis, totally unsuitable for these strenuous physical events.]

Water Olympics begin with:
1. Rabbi Fishbone as M.C..

2. Runner approaches Torch Area. Runner is a bearded Rabbi carrying a lighted torch. He then runs up the steps leading to the depository torch holder. Somehow the steps break, and he falls down, dropping the torch, setting the wooden steps on fire.

3. The White Lake fire truck is standing by, and the firemen spring into action putting the flames out.

4. The runner gets up; relights his torch, then lights the main torch.

5. The crowd applauds this ceremony.

6. The Kletzmer band starts off the Olympics by playing the national anthem.

7. In the background, behind the athlete's area, some local thugs, grab Rabbi Gross, and kidnap him. One of the bullies, removes the number on the Rabbi,and puts it on. When he is changing his clothes we observe his physique to be identical to Arnold Schwarzenager. He then puts on a fake beard. He tapes up Rabbi Gross and carries him away under his arm, who is violently kicking, and placed in a parked van.

8. When the judges and other Rabbis see the imposter, they go into a panic.

9. "Everything is lost! Now everyone will bet on

the imposter, and we will be bankrupted

10. " Solly says, "Don't worry, the bum is not going to win!"

[During the announcer's broadcasting, he errors in his pronunciation by accidentally saying,"Vite Lake, I mean White Lake."]

[T.V. News Bulletin-Local Rabbi in White Lake N.Y., Sullivan County, has put together an exciting water Olympics for charity purposes this Sunday, in this small town, not far from the site of the original Woodstock concert in Bethel.

11. Rabbi Fishbone then begins to introduce the contestants.He reads off their names and backgrounds, and when he gets to number one, the bully, he exclaims "Oy vay!"

12. When the people see his size and physique,a long line starts to form at the one hundred dollar "donation both" to cash in on number one. When Solly sees what's happening he grabs the mike and orders "all windows are closed, I repeat, all donations have ended!"

13. The Rabbis in the contestant area are murmuring, and panicking. "Vot are we going to do? Instead of raising money, we are going to lose our whole synagogue!. Solly tries to calm them down and repeats," that bum is not going to win our Olympics,not if I can help it!"

14. The contestants are all lined up at the edge of the lake to begin the race. Tensions mount in the crowd!

15. When T.V. camerman scans from left to right, he comes to stop on number 1, and says "where did that monster come from?"

16. A helicopter flies low, and the camerman inside announces, "It looks like the big race is about to begin!"

17. Rabbi Fishbone announces that the race is about to begin. He then explains the sequence of events, as follows:

First the men will wait for the starter's gun. Then they will swim to the five rafts.Then, once they are on the rafts, they will jump onto their jet skis. The course is marked off on the lake with floating flags. After they pass the last flag, they will circle back to the rafts, and put on their water skis. Now in the water, they will be pulled down the lake by speedboats. During this segment of the race, there are ramps to be skied over, shooting them up into the air. A close up on the ramps reveal the other bullies sabotaging the angle of the ramps to an impossible high angle.This will shoot our contestants high into the air, causing them to crash into the water. They do not alter their co-conspirators' ramp. Then, after they complete the water ski course, they will remove their skis, and run the track to the finish line.

18.All during the race, announcers at different Locations, give exciting up to date reports of who is winning, and calamity reports of accidents and crashes.

19. Solly and Goyshan try desperately to knock number one out of the race.

20. [Rabbi's wife,scolding.Insert where appropriate.]

    RABBI'S WIFE
You shouldn't be betting! Betting is a sin!

    RABBI
I'm not betting or gambling! I'm making a "donation!" See, look at the sign. It says "DONATION".

21. Special camera treatment [fast speed] will create scenes reminiscent of the old black and white films involving chases and close calls. Slow and fast motion can have a field day!

[All of our Rabbis will be wearing the long sleeves and long legged striped bathing suits of the 20's and 30's.]

22. During the final foot race, Goyshan drops out, exhausted. Number one is in the lead, pursued by Solly. With his last energies, Solly catches up, throws his arms around number one's waist yelling, "the bum is not going to win!, the bum is not going to win!"

[Cut to Solly's bedroom, where Solly is in bed, his arms around a pillow.]

SOLLY
The bum is not going to win! The bum is not going to win!

[It is at this point that it becomes apparent that the whole W.L.O. never happened.]
[Solly opens his eyes, looks around, and gives a sigh of relief, realizing that W.L.O. was just a nightmare.]

FADE OUT

FADE IN

[Solly is walking through kitchen door, starts to go outside, but stops and turns around when he hears phone ringing.]

SOLLY
Hello. Solly here. [Concerned look on his face.]

JULIE'S VOICE
She's gone! (Crying) Solly, she's gone!

                    SOLLY
Who's gone?

          JULIE'S VOICE (Sarcastically)
You're daughter! This morning she wasn't in her
bed....She left me a note.

          SOLLY (Panicky)
Read it! Read it!

          JULIE'S VOICE (With sobs and tears.)
Dear Mommy: Don't worry! Please tell daddy that I
am going to be a real snowbird! I'm flying to
visit him in White Lake on a Greyhound bus! I
will arrive at the N.Y. Port Authority bus
terminal on Wednesday morning, at about eleven
A.M.. Love Kimmy!
(Continuing) She took money from my bag! (Full of
anger.) Maybe eighty dollars.

          SOLLY
(Trying to keep composed)
[Close-up on Solly's face]
Don't worry,Julie! Don't worry! She will be
alright! G-d is looking over her. She's a smart
girl. I'll be at the bus terminal tomorrow
morning, and I promise you that I will call you
as soon as she arrives.

          JULIE
But she is such a little girl! Anything can
happen! Should I call the police? Do they have
radios or cell phones on the bus? Maybe they can
locate the bus she is on, and the driver can tell
us if she is o.k.? Which bus line was it/ Oh yes,
she said it was Greyhound.

          SOLLY
Look. I'll call the bus company, and tell them
what happened. When they locate her I will
immediately call you. O.K.?

          JULIE (Angry)
It's all your fault! You put all these "Snowbird"
ideas in her head.

                         107

            SOLLY
Goodbye!
[Puts the phone down.]
(Out loud,looking up. He is talking to G-d)
She wants to be a real Snowbird!

            GOYSHAN
[Comes in from the outside.]
Is there anything wrong?
[Special effects on background music. Volume
starts very low, then gradually gets louder and
louder.Music is Jewish Freylich.Fast and lively.]
            SOLLY
[Goes into a little dance.]
Guess who is coming to White Lake?

            GOYSHAN
Who?
            SOLLY
A little Snowbird!

            GOYSHAN
[Questioning look, then facial expression changes
to surprise, as he catches on.]
(With joy and happiness) A little Snowbird!
[He grabs Solly's hands, and is now dancing with
him.]
            SOLLY
Yes! My Kimmy! She took a Greyhound bus, and is
now on her way to the Port Authority bus terminal
In N.Y.City, and she should arrive tomorrow!

            GOYSHAN
Kimmy is coming here? I don't believe it!

            SOLLY
Yeah! But first I have to make some phone calls.
[Goes over to phone.] Hello Greyhound? Do you
have a bus arriving from Miami, tomorrow morning,
around eleven A.M.? You do? Great! Let me tell
you what happened. My little daughter, Kimmy...

Sound and Visual FADE OUT

FADE IN [On interior of bus which has just
stopped at a restaurant. Driver is putting radio
earphones down.]

                BUS DRIVER (Talking to himself)
So we have a small "Snowbird on board!"
Let's take a look.
[Gets up, and slowly makes his way down the isle
Towards the rear of the bus, looking for Kimmy. He
Spots her.
[Close up on Kimmy, sleeping, curled up like a
kitten. He takes blanket out from overhead
compartment, and gently places it on Kimmy. He
returns to his driver's seat, picks up the radio,
and speaks into the mike.]
Yeah! I've got her! She's sleeping like a baby.
Tell her parents not to worry. I'll keep an eye
on her until we get to New York.

Cut to: Solly on the phone
[Tremendous sigh of relief with accompanying body
language.]

                SOLLY
Hello, Julie? Good news! They've located our
Snowbird on the bus, Miami to N.Y.City Express.
Don't worry! I'll be at the Port Authority
terminal way before it pulls in, waiting! As soon
as I have her in my arms I will call you! O.K.?

                JULIE
[On phone]O.K.! O.K.! This was all your fault,
Solly! You put the idea into her head to be a
Snowbird, to live in White Lake, to go fishing
and boating with you everyday…She's now going to
miss her school classes!

                SOLLY
(Starting to get a little annoyed)
I am not going to let you blame this thing on me.
Maybe her school play had something to do with
it? Anyway, the holiday season is almost here,
and school will be closed.

                JULIE
Call me as soon as she arrives. [Hangs up.]

SOLLY
[As soon as Solly hangs up phone it rings again.]

MOLLY   (On phone)
Solly, is that you? Your line was busy, and I am
going out of my mind worrying about Kimmy.
(Yelling!) Julie just told me that you let Kimmy
take a bus, by herself, all the way to New York.
Are you mashugger?

SOLLY
Don't worry, Mom. I just spoke to the bus
company, and she is alright. I will call you as
soon as she arrives!

FADE OUT

FADE IN
[Early morning scene, pan of beautiful White
Lake, then to front of Solly's house. Solly and
Goyshan are leaving the house and are getting
into Solly's SUV.]

GOYSHAN [Inside vehicle.]
I still can't believe she is making the whole
trip on her own!

SOLLY
[Starts up vehicle, and puts country music
station on. He pulls out onto route 55]

RADIO D.J.
Hi, you all! It won't be long now, to find out
who will be the winner of our Mountain Music
Song writing contest. So many beautiful songs
have been submitted! It is going to be a tough
job picking the winner!

[Special Aerial Camera Coverage]
Camera covers trip from White Lake to N.Y.City.
Traveling along Route 17, before and over
Wursboro Mountain, thru the toll boths in
Harriman, getting onto the NY Thruway, down the
Palisades Parkway, over the George Washington

Bridge, down the West Side Highway, and finally
pulling into the Port Authority area.]
[Country music, playing the whole trip.]

        SOLLY
[Gets out of the SUV, leaving Goyshan to watch,
goes into the terminal, goes over to the Coffee-
Bakery counter, and comes out with bagels and two
coffees in his hands. He then gets into his
vehicle and divides up the food with Goyshan.]

[Looks at his watch.]
Only thirty minutes until Kimmy's bus arrives.
This whole thing has got me nervous!

        GOYSHAN
Calm down, Solly! I'm a little twichy too, but
It's going to be great seeing Kimmy!

[Special Camera Action]
View lifts up from terminal building, goes out
across the Hudson River, onto the Jersey
Turnpike, and then travels down the turnpike. Our
camera picks up the Greyhound bus, as it passes
by the Newark Airport exit coming north.

Camera Zooms in on bus.

Cut TO: Inside of bus, on Kimmy, sitting on bus
driver's lap.Looks like she is driving the bus.

        BUS DRIVER
Listen, Snowbird. You know your father is waiting
for you at the termina?

        KIMMY
[She has her hands on the steering wheel.]
Uh-huh!

        BUS DRIVER
You know what you did was wrong! Scaring your
mother and father, and anyway, you cn't be a real
Snowbird! You are not a real Snowbird because you
Got everything backwards! Snowbirds don't fly
North in the autumn and winter time.
(Emphatically) They fly South!

111

                KIMMY
[Frowning, and almost in tears, she doesn't like
what the driver just told her.]

[Shot, from inside bus, looking out front window.
Bus going into the Lincoln Tunnel,coming out, and
going up special ramp into bus terminal.When the
bus stops, and the doors open, we see Solly and
Goyshan at the curb, waiting.]

[New camera angle.
Shot taken from behind Solly and Goyshan.]

                KIMMY
[She is wrapped up in blanket from bus, because
it is a little chilly. She has her hands to her
eyes from crying. She leaps into Solly's arms!]

Daddy, I'm so glad to see you! I was afraid, the
whole trip, that you would be angry, and not meet
me here. How do Snowbirds do it? It's such a long
trip! (Crying) The bus driver said that I am not
a real Snowbird, only a naughty run-away girl!

                SOLLY
{Solly is kissing and caressing her, while
Goyshan takes a sweatshirt from under his arm,
and gives it to Solly to put on Kimmy.

                KIMMY
[While Solly is putting on sweatshirt]
Hi Rabbi Goyshan....Is the bus driver right?

                GOYSHAN
(Hesitates his answer) Errr...(Looks at Solly, not
knowing what to say.)

[Kimmy is now walking toward SUV, in between
Solly and Goyshan]

                SOLLY
[Nods his head to Goyshan. Winks his eye.]

                GOYSHAN
Why..yes! (Very emphatically!) Kimmy, you are

                              112

definitely a beautiful government certified, approved Snowbird. You see, you qualify to be a Snowbird because, sometimes a Snowbird has a Special mission and has to return North to accomplish it!

[All get into SUV. Kimmy is starting to feel better,but very tired, stops crying, and puts her head on Goyshan's lap.]

          KIMMY [Starts to fall asleep,]
A special mission? I wonder what my special mission is?

          SOLLY
(Very softly! Puts his finger to his lips.)
I'll be right back. I have to make two, very important phone calls.

[Close up on Kimmy's head, on Goyshan's lap.]

          FADE OUT

          FADE IN
[To Kimmy's room in Solly's house in White Lake.]

[Kimmy is trying on winter clothing from boxes next to her bed. Then, when she is all dressed, she enters the kitchen where Solly and Goyshan are having coffee. The radio is on, playing country music.]

          KIMMY
Good morning Daddy! Good morning Rabbi Goyshan!
[She goes over to each one, and kisses them on their cheek]
Can I go outside to see the lake? Can we go for a speed boat ride?

          SOLLY
Hold on Kimmy! First you have to have some breakfast.

          KIMMY

[Kimmy sits down at table, and puts napkin around her neck.]

          SOLLY
Guess what we are having for breakfast?

          KIMMY
(Curiously) What? Scrambled eggs?

          SOLLY
[Uncovering a stack of pancakes, Kimmy's favorite!]
Pancakes!

          KIMMY
Thank you Daddy!

          GOYSHAN
[Close up. Rubbing his hands together, like an excited child.]
I just love pancakes!

                    FADE OUT

                    FADE IN
[Goyshan, Kimmy and Solly are getting int Solly's speedboat. Boat has Kimmy's name on sides and back.]

[Everyone is having a great time,enjoying the beautiful autumn weather, the beautiful lake surrounded by breathtaking color painted trees.]

[Solly was especially happy because he never had Kimmy with him before, to share G-d's creations.]

          SOLLY
[Looks up toward the sky.]
Thank you G-d, please don't let this happiness end.
[Distant shot of speedboat tearing up the lake, then normal shots of Solly waving to his friends On the waterfront.]
[As they approach Rabbi Fishbone's dock, Solly slows down, and it glides along side the dock, where the Rabbi is fishing with his daughter

                    114

Rivkah. She is about the same age as Kimmy.]

        KIMMY
(Thinking to herself.]
Off Stage:
How lucky Rivkah is, to be able to live on this
beautiful lake all year round!

        SOLLY
(Yelling.)Hi Rabbi! This is my daughter Kimmy!
She's visiting from Florida.
        KIMMY
[Waving and yelling.]
Hello Rabbi! Hello Rivkah![Turning towards
Goyshan.]Is he a real Rabbi,like you?
        GOYSHAN
(Dumbfounded look on his face.He doesn't know
what to answer.He then nods his head
affirmatively.]

[Pull away from dock, shot,as Solly drives back
onto lake.]

        FADE OUT

        FADE IN

[Kimmy's bedroom.]
[Solly and Kimmy are lying on bed reading book.]

OFF STAGE:
[Jewish Music-"Sunrise,Sunset."]

        SOLLY
Let's start here, "Introduction To The High
Holidays."
Kimmy, do you know that the holly days start with
"Rosh Hashonnah",the Jewish New Year? Kimmy, do
you know what year we are in?

        KIMMY
Sue I know. That's easy! The year that we are in
is 2012!

        SOLLY
No, I mean what is the Jewish year we are in?

                KIMMY
I'm sorry,Daddy I don't know. Mommy never talked
to me about these things.

                SOLLY
Let's see…, this year was 5772. That means we are
going into 5773!

                KIMMY
5772? 5773? [Thinking..] How could that be? Where
did..[Thinking..]3760 more years come from?

                SOLLY
[Thinking very hard.]
I've got it! We Jewish people started counting
the years beginning from Adam and Eve, down
through Abraham, Issac, Jacob and Moses, who
received the Torah (Bible)from G-d on Mount
Sinai, until the destruction of the second Temple
by the Romans which was in the year 3760.Then the
current era began which started about 2012 years
ago. Together, beggining fromand Eve we have a
history of 5772 years.

                FADE OUT

                FADE IN

Exterior
[White Lake Synagogue]
[Sun is setting.]

OFF STAGE:
[Sound of Shofar blowing.]
[After last blast of shofah, we hear happy
voices of congregents wishing their friends
and family "a Happy and Healthy New Year."

[Interior of Synagogue]
Camera zooms in on stained glass window
with giant size Jewish Star of David.]

OFF STAGE:
Cantor's voice singing "Kol Nidrei."

        FADE OUT

        FADE IN

[Solly's house-Interior, Living Room.]

        RABBI FISHBONE
[Close up]
[Seated around him is his daughter
Rivkah,Solly,and Goyshan.]

[Everyone is leaning towards the Rabbi to hear
his words on the 'Laws of Succoth."

[He is giving a class on the commandment "to take
the four parts of the luluv". This commandment is
necessary to celebrate the holiday of "Succoth".
Along with this important commandment is the
commandment "to dwell in Booths".]

Each person is required to own a "Luluv Set"!
What does this set consist of? I have an idea!.
Let's all go to my friend Schlomo. He is holding
my Luluv set. I still have to select an Esrog.

        KIMMY
What's an Esrog Rabbi?

        RIVKAH
[Before her father can answer, she jumps in and
explains.]

It's a citrus fruit...like a lemon, and it smells
so wonderful!.

        EVERYONE
[They all get into Solly's SUV.]

[Inside SUV}

        RABBI FISHBONE

To continue, the Esrog is one of the four items
necessary to complete the set.

          GOYSHAN
What are the other three items?

          RABBI FISHBONE
Next, we must pick out an undamaged Palm Branch.
The Palm Branch is the backbone of the set. After
we place it in the center of the other two plant
species, the Myrtle and the Willow, the Luluv set
will be complete.
When we get to Schlomo's I will show you how the
set looks finished.

          RIVKAH
Then we wave the Luluv a certain way! I will show
you how to do this later.

          RABBI FISHBONE
[He directs Solly the way to Schlomo's Sukkah
factory.]

          FADE OUT
[On Solly's SUV driving down the road.]

          FADE IN
Exterior Sukkah Factory.

[Solly's SUV pulling into driveway. Everyone gets
out,and they are greeted by Schlomo.]

          SCHLOMO
Good Yuntiv! Good Yuntov! Sholom Alechem! How are
you Rabbi? [Goes over to shake his hand.]
I have your Luluv set, and I just got in a
shipment of beautiful Morocan Estrogen! You will
have the priviledge of first choice!

[Everyone enters into store.]

          SOLLY
(Proudly.)

Schlomo, I've decided to build a Sukkah! The
wood, I'm getting from the lunber yard, but I
need the bamboo for the roof. Can you show me
what you have?

        SCHOLMO
How big will your Sukkah be?

        SOLLY
[Thinking. Trying to figure it out in his head.]
Can I trouble you for a pencil and paper?

[While Solly is doing his calculations, we pan to
the girls, who are picking up Esrogen, and
examining them.Rivkah is explaining to Kimmy, how
to check for imperfections. Goyshan is also
handling them, and puts one to his nose, smelling
it's beautiful aroma. He reacts to his long
inhale by swooning.]

        SOLLY
(Towards Schlomo.Yells out, because he finally
figured out the dimensions.)
Sixteen feet by eight feet!

        SCHLOMO
That's easy! All you need are two rolls of bamboo
mats. [Starts writing up the order.]
And how many Luluv sets?

        SOLLY
(Quickly answers.) Five sets!

        KIMMY
How come, Daddy? There are only three of us. You,
me, and Goyshan!

        SOLLY
Oops! I let the cat out of the bag. It was to be
a surprise! Your mother and Nuna are coming here
to White Lake, for Sukkos. I'm picking them up at
the airport the day after tomorrow!

        KIMMY
[Kimmy's face is at first happy, but then her
expression changes because she realizes she will
have to return to Florida with them.]

119

(Sad and softly.)
Oh….

          FADE OUT
[Schlomo loading the bamboo onto the roof of
Solly's SUV.]

OFF STAGE

          RABBI FISHBONE
Solly, tomorrow, I'll send over Rabbi Gross, with
an instruction book, which will help you build
your Sukkah.

          FADE IN
[On truck from lumberyard, pulling away from
Solly's driveway. Remaining on the ground is a
pile of two by fours, and 12 sheets of plywood,
eight feet by four feet each]

          SOLLY,GOYSHAN,& RABBI GROSS [Little Person]
[All are talking.Solly is strutting around,
trying to figure out the best spot to erect the
Sukkah. He keeps looking up at the sky, because
Rabbi Fishbone told him that there must not be
anything overhanging, which might obstruct the
view, through the bamboo.]

          SOLLY
This is the spot! But there is a branch sticking
out! The Rabbi said we must be able to see the
stars through the bamboo, but that big branch
will be blocking our view!

          GOYSHAN
Don't worry,Solly! Rabbi Gross and I will take
care of the branch! You go inside, and make Kimmy
her breakfast. Rabbi Gross and I will set up the
frame of the Sukkah.

          SOLLY
[Leaves the two, and goes into the house.]
O.K.! Thank you.

          RABBI GROSS

[Holding the instruction book in his little
hands.]
(Reading out loud to Goyshan.)

        GOYSHAN
[His back is towards the little Rabbi. He is
nailing together the two by fours, which will be
the base. He then puts them in place and fastens
the upright two by fours in place, leaving a
skeleton of the Sukkah. All that has to be done
now, is to cut the tops off to their proper
height. Rabbi Gross is in charge of the buz saw,
and is using a string and marker to mark off
where these beams are to be cut. Goyshan returns
to the instruction book, with his back to the
Sukkah. Goyshan reads out loud…]
"The height of the Sukkah should not be less than
twentyone handwiths. (Turns his head towards
Rabbi Gross for an instant, then back.)
Hear that little Rabbi Rabbi? Twentyone
handwiths.Count them out loud to me!

        RABBI GROSS
(Counts out loud, while putting one hand over the
other. When he gets to twentyone, he makes a
mark. Then Goyshan turns around and helps him,
with a string to mark off each upright beam.

        GOYSHAN
[Turns around,picks up the circular saw, and cuts
off the tops of each upright. He doesn't realize
what he just did until he lays the top beams
across.! He goes into a panic when this
realization sets in!]

        FADE OUT
[On Solly calling the lumberyard for another
delivery.]

        FADE IN
[Solly, Goyshan,Rabbi Gross and Kimmy.]

        SOLLY
[Solly is securing the walls of the Sukkah,
against the frame, using a loud nail gun. As he

121

finishes the last nail, he turns towards Goyshan]
O.K. Goyshan, it's time for you to put the bamboo
on the roof.

GOYSHAN
I've got an idea! Come here Rabbi Gross!
[He lifts him up, and puts him on his shoulders.]

RABBI GROSS
O.K.! Solly. Hand me up the bamboo rolls!
[He then lays the bamboo in place.]
Goyshan, hand me the power saw!
[He then cuts down the overhanging branch.]

SOLLY
Kimmy, please come here! Now comes the fun part.
[Solly opens a box filled with beautiful shiney
decorations.Kimmy, Goyshan and Rabbi Gross put up
the decorations.]

GOYSHAN
[He goes into the house and carries out the table
and chairs, from the kitchen, into the Sukkah.]

FADE OUT
[With everyone inside, Rabbi Gross recites the
prayer "To dwell in the Sukkah."]
Everyone, "Amen!"

FADE IN
[Sukkah] Interior
[Everyone is inside.Each person has their Luluv
in their hand,while Rabbi Fishbone recites the
prayer, everyone repeats it. They then wave the
Luluv as the Rabbi demonstrates.After this
ceremony, Molly and Julie bring the food into the
Sukkah.]

EVERYONE
[Singing, eating, and having a good time]

FADE OUT

FADE IN

[Scene at the airport. Kimmy is hugging and kissing Solly and Goyshan goodbye. She is thanking Solly for such a good time, and making her a real "Snowbird". She understands now, what Goyshan told her. That she was a real "Snowbird" because she was on a "special mission". She has come to the realization that her "special mission" was to learn about her Jewish heritage, about observing and keeping the High Holidays, especially the celebration of Sukkos!]

    SOLLY
Solly reassures her, that he loves her, and will be visiting her shortly.

    KIMMY
Daddy...I have a confession to make to you. You know, the whole story, about me wanting to be a real "Snowbird"... about me running away from home, well I kind of told a white lie!

    SOLLY
What do you mean?

    KIMMY
Well,... I used the Snowbird story as an excuse to run away. My real reason was to be with you! [She throws her arms around Solly. [Close-up on Kimmy's face, showing her tears rolling down her checks.]
I don't want to leave you daddy!

    SOLLY
[Trying to console her.]
Listen, sweetheart...I'll be flying down to you shortly! See..[He pulls out a whole book of airline tickets.]
Cheaper by the dozen!...[To change the subject.] Tell me what you want for Chanukah, cause that's when I'm coming down to see you. That's only sixty days from today! That's not too bad!Is it?

    KIMMY
[Wiping away her tears.]
I guess not.

            SOLLY
[Whispering] And even if you made up the whole
story, I want you to know that I love you, and
that I think you are the most wonderful
"Snowbird" in the whole world! [Kisses Kimmy.]

            FADE OUT

            FADE IN
Solly's house.   Interior

[Solly is on the phone speaking to the manager of
Jewish Towers,(Molly's building)in Florida.]

Off Stage:

We are sorry, Mr.Batimo! You must come down here
immediately! Or we will be forced to place your
mother in a state mental facility in Gainesville!

            SOLLY
O.K.! O.K.! I'll be right down to discuss this
with you in two days! Don't do anything!
[Panicking. Turns to Goyshan.]
Listen, my friend. [Put his arm around him.]
There's a little problem with Molly in Florida. I
have to leave you alone. Could you watch the fort
for me, for a few days, until I return? Do you
think you can manage?

            GOYSHAN
[Nods his head.] Don't worry, my friend,I'll take
good care of everything.

            SOLLY
Do you think you could drive me to the airport,
tomorrow morning?

FADE OUT

        FADE IN
[Inside airplane. Solly is sitting next to the
window again, thinking, drinking, worrying about
what he will encounter at Jewish Towers.]

        FADE OUT

        FADE IN
[Solly is coming through the front doors of
Jewish Towers, into the main lobby, and walks
over to the reception desk, where he greets the
manager, Mrs.Goodman.]

        MRS. GOODMAN
Mr. Batimo! I'm so glad to see you! Your mother
has become a severe problem to this facility!.
Last week, we had our required monthly fire
drill, and your mother didn't respond! She was
inside her apartment, sleeping, probably from her
medication. Our special fire alarm rang in her
apartment, and she didn't wake up and leave! We
called her on her telephone, to no avail. We then
sent one of our managers to knock on her door.
She knocked on her door for five minutes
straight. We then used our master key to enter.
Your mom was fast asleep. When she came down to
get her mail, the next day, she began
halucinating. She claims the super, sneaks into
her apartment each night, and steels her
belongings. She claims he sends up sleeping gas
through the vents, like in the T.V. program
"Mission Impossibe", then he waits for her to be
knocked out, and enters her apartment. She claims
he stole her fishing rod, and her valueable
antique glass ash trays. Our in-house doctor, has
evaluated your mother to be suffering from an
advanced case of Paranoia, Dementia, and
Altzheimer's desease!

        SOLLY
Don't worry, Mrs.Goodman! I'll speak with Molly.
I'll take care of everything! Maybe I'll have to

                    125

stay here with her, for a few days.

        MRS.GOODMAN
I don't think that staying here with her for a
few days will be sufficient! You will have to
make the necessary arrangements for Molly to
leave! It's in the lease!

        SOLLY
Let me visit with her for a few days, and then I
will tell you what I am going to do.[Solly goes
into the elevator, and presses the button.]

        FADE OUT

        FADE IN
[Molly's apartment]

        SOLLY

[Talking to Kimmy on his cell phone.]
Kimmy, darling. Believe it or not, I'm at Nuna's
apartment. We have had an emergency!

        KIMMY
(Concerned) Is Nuna o.k.?

        SOLLY
[Not wanting to cause Kimmy any alarm.]
She's fine, darling. I had to come down to see
Nuna because her lease was up, and she decided to
move back to White Lake. That way I can help her
with her shopping and cooking. One thing which I
have to ask you for, is your forgiveness…

        KIMMY
What do I have to forgive you for,Daddy?

        SOLLY
You see…sweetheart, I will not be able to see you
this trip! I will be tied up with making the
move, and arrangements for Nuna. Please forgive
me. I love you. I will call you when I get home .
Also, regards from Goyshan.

        KIMMY
I understand. Please kiss Nuna goodbye, from me.
Have a safe trip, Daddy. See you Channukah time.

        FADE OUT

        FADE IN
Solly's house, Exterior,side door.
[Back shot. Solly and Molly are approaching the
side door, and Goyshan is coming out of the door
to greet them. Goyshan gives Molly a big hug.
They all enter the house.

        FADE OUT

OFF STAGE:
Molly's voice.(Annoyed)
When are you going to bring me my piano?

        FADE IN
[Living room. Molly, Solly, and Goyshan are
seated.]

[Sound. Country music from radio.]

        MOLLY
Solly,…it's been four weeks since I left Florida.
It's so cold up here! [She is bundled-up with
multiple heavy sweaters.] And I still don't have
my piano!..And the radio only plays country
music! Solly, please take me to the bank, I have
to transfer my checking account and Social
Security check to White Lake.

        FADE OUT

``   FADE IN
[Moving van has just stopped in front of house.
Three men get out, and proceed to unload Molly's
piano. Goyshan is outside, supervising the move.
Somehow, as they are bringing in the piano, he

                   127

gets pinned in between the piano and the doorway.
After going through a lot of struggling and
contortions, he manages to squeeze out.The piano
is moved into the living room to the spot Molly
shows them.]

MOLLY
[The men leave, and Molly is overcome with joy!
It's like seeing an old friend again. She sits
down on the piano seat, and plays a very happy
tune. After another piece, she begins to play
"Poems", Solly's favorite!]

This is for you, my chochucolu.

SOLLY
[Close-up.] Facial expression on his face is one
of happiness, indicating his approval and
happiness to again enjoy this piece. He is also
happy because he has brought back tranquility to
his mother.

GOYSHAN
[Close-up.] Facial expression on his face, of
happiness, to hear Solly's favorite piece.

GOYSHAN & SOLLY
[Camera]
[Special care is taken to synchronize their head
movements to the tempo of the music.]

Both men are enjoying Molly's playing. Goyshan is
using a pencil as a baton. Both men are looking
at each other. The bars of the music are
approaching when Molly always makes her playing
error. Both men start to crunch-up their facial
expressions, and body language beccause Molly is
coming to the spot which she always misplays,
but then… an amazing thing happens! Molly plays
the piece perfect! No repeating! No fumbling! No
going back! They are astonished! They both look
hard, at each other.

SOLLY
[Motions Goyshan to follow him into the kitchen.]

(Speaking softly.)
Did you just hear, what I just heard? Did you see
that? She played it perfectly! Somethings fishey!
My whole life I've listened to my mother play
this piece, and she never got it right!

        GOYSHAN
Let's go back into the living room. I'm going to
ask her to play Poems again!

        SOLLY
O.K., but just act casual.

[Solly and Goyshan casually walk back into living
room.]

        GOYSHAN
Molly. You didn't play Solly's favorite
piece,Poems, yet. Could you please play it for
me, too?

        MOLLY
No problem, it will be my pleasure, Rabbi.
[Absent minded gesture.]

(To herself.) I thought I played it before.
O.K.! Here goes.
[She places the sheet music in front.]

[Solly and Goyshan look at each other in
anticipation, communicating with eye contact,and
facial expressions.]

        MOLLY
[As Molly begins to play, both men are moving
their hands to the music.]

        SOLLY & GOYSHAN
[As the music approaches the critical bars of
music, which Molly never plays correctly,Solly
grabs his earlobe as a sign to Goyshan to listen
closely.]

            MOLLY
(Molly plays it perfectly, again!)

            SOLLY & GOYSHAN
[Both make exclaimation gestures, immediately
after this part is finished.]

            SOLLY
[He motions Goyshan, to follow him into the
kitchen again.]

(Whispering)I think we just made a big discovery!

            GOYSHAN
[Nodding his head in agreement.]

            SOLLY
Do you remember what you told me about "Cross-
Over Angels", on the airplane, when we first met?
How, sometimes,sometimes, maybe in a million
cross-overs, they might slip up? I think we both
witnessed that million to one ..mistake! Molly
has crossed over!

            GOYSHAN
What? What do you mean? (Nervously.) Molly is an
angel?

            SOLLY
[Puts his finger to his lips.] Shooosh!

            MOLLY
(Annoyed)Something's not right! It's the pitch!
Solly,tomorrow I want you to find me a piano
tuner. O.K.?

            GOYSHAN
[Sneaks-up behind Molly, and examines her. First,
her back left side, and then examines her back
right side. He then goes over to Solly .]

(Whispering.) She looks the same to me!

        SOLLY
That's right! She's suppose to look the same. My
mother has crossed over into the next world. No
pain, no suffering,just like you said! In a
split second, my mother is not Molly, anymore,
but a cross-over angel! And now, you and I are
living with an angel!

[Solly goes over to the couch, falls on it, and
collapses, arms and legs spread out. Goyshan
follows suit.]

        Solly
I've got a great idea. In order to confirm our
suspicions, let's invite the Rabbi over,(Rabbi
Fishbone)to see if he detects anything fishy.

        Goyshan
That's very funny, what you just said..Rabbi
Fishbone,anything fishy! (Accentuates the words
Fishbone, and fishy)(laughter)

        Solly
(Annoyed) Common, Goyshan, get serious! This is a
very serious matter! Maybe we are wrong about
Molly?

[Solly goes over to the wall phone and dials
Rabbi Fishbone.]

Hellow Rabbi. How are you feeling today? Good!
Yes,I called to find out if you might be able to
come over for a few minutes. We have a personal
problem, here, with my mom-Molly. No, she's not
sick, but we think she is not herself!

        Goyshan
[Laughing, then covers mouth as not to be heard.]

        Solly
Thank you, thank you, Rabbi! Molly will be very
happy to see you. See you you in ten minutes.

Fade-Out to Fade-In on Goyshan and Solly walking

towards front door, and opening it.

        Goyshan and Solly
Welcome,welcome, come on right in!

        Solly
Rabbi, please take a close look at Molly, and
tell me if she seems different.

        Rabbi Fishbone
(Quietly to Solly)Different? How different?
{Rabbi slowly circles Molly, sitting at piano,
studying her, while holding his magnifying glass
close to his eye]

        Molly
Rabbi, let me play for you. What is your
favorite?

(Solly jumps into the conversation) Mom, could
you play my favorite piece, "Poems" for the
Rabbi?

        Molly
Thank you Solly, for picking this song. (Turning
towards Rabbi)it's also one of my favorites.
[Molly begins playing…] and a serene quiet comes
over our living room scene. Goyshan, Solly, and
the Rabbi, are leaning towards Molly. at the
piano. Solly and Goyshan are getting more uptight
as Molly's fingers glide closer and closer toward
that terrible , earbending crash and clash of
incorrect notes. Solly and Goyshan cringe up,
waiting for her error, which will indicate that
she hasn't cross-over, then look and smile at
each other, realizing as an angel, she will play
it perfectly. So the cringe is gone,and they are
prepared for a quiet, smooth ending to "Poems"

(But the error does happen! Molly hits the wrong
notes, and Solly and Goyshan ,totally surprised,
look at each other, completely confused.She then,
as always, goes back, and corrects her misplayed
notes with the right notes.)

         Rabbi Fishbone
Molly, Molly, that was beautiful, with tears
rolling down his cheeks

         FADE OUT

[Molly playing at the piano]

         FADE IN

[This scene depicts the deteriation of Solly's
fond relationship with his mother, Molly. Molly
starts accusing him of hiding her medication, and
stealing her check book, which later turns up
where she hid it, under her mattress! This is due
to her Alzheimers'. She hides her possessions,
then forgets where she put them Then the cue-de-
gra comes when she puts on her winter slacks, and
sees that they are four sizes too big. She
accuses Solly of cutting her waistbands.
Actually, she has lost twentyfive pounds since
she last wore her slacks, eighteen years earlier!
Solly swears to her that he is innocent, then
starts to lose his temper, but he catches himself
when he reminds himself, that he is dealing with
an angel!]

         MOLLY
[Molly goes over to the flower vase on top of the
piano, to remove the wilted, dead flowers.]

Solly,(angry) don't buy me live flowers anymore!
Only buy dead flowers, (she means artificial)
They are just as pretty, and they never die! (We
can read into her words, maybe a little
symbolism.?)

[Camera follows Molly into kitchen where she
throws flowers into the trash. Close-up on
flowers in trash.]

Solly, I can't live here anymore! Take me to the
Senior Citizens' country club. I want to check it

out. I really want to be able to play their Grand Piano, whenever I want! It has such a beautiful tone! (Really called "The White Lake Nursing Home")

FADE OUT

FADE IN

[White Lake Nursing Home.-Exterior]

[Solly is carrying her luggage into the front door.]

FADE OUT on door closing.

FADE IN-EXTERIOR
[Our view is filled with bright spring blossoms Aound the shore of White Lake. Then ...out, onto the surface of the lake, which reflects the beautiful blue sky. Then ,up, onto a flock of geese flying north]

CUT TO-RV Village of Del Ray Beach
[Jeffrey and Sandra are getting into their RV, waving goodbye to their winter friends,who are holding their luggage, and are also heading north. back home)

JEFFREY
(Coursely) Where is your winter coat?

SANDRA
It's, (thinking...cannot remember, since they have been in Florida for over five months.)
(Bluffing!) It's back in White Lake!

JEFFREY

(Yelling) No dummy! You brought it down here. Go
back into the house and check out the closets!

        SANDRA
[Sandra goes back into building..]

        SOLLY
        [While waiting in vehicle he is admiring
his new Rolex watch. His auto insurance covered
his loss.]

        SANDRA
[Returns to vehicle carrying her winter coat.
Gets into vehicle.]

        JEFFREY
(Smart Alec quality to his voice.)
Ah hah...(dragging out hah.)

        SANDRA
[Shooting through windshield head-on]

(Not willing to admit defeat, defiant, she
turns to Jeffrey.)
You know it all...so where are the house keys?

        FADE OUT

FADE IN-Inside Solly's House, White Lake

        GOYSHAN
Solly, can I borrow your SUV ? My leg is
killing me. (Faking a limp.)
I'd like to visit Dr.Chan. I think my ghaut is
acting up again!

        SOLLY
(Hands Goyshan his keys.) Remember to take it easy
on Route seventeen!
The cops are patroling it like crazy!

        CUT TO – Exterior of Tuxedo Store

(Goyshan pulls up with his vehicle. Then gets
out, approaches entrance, suspiciously, looks
quickly to his left, then to his right before he

enters store.)

      FADE OUT

      FADE IN-EXTERIOR, Molly's Nursing Home, Sun
setting.

      SOLLY
(Solly is kissing Molly goodnight at front door.
He turns around, goes down the stairs over to his
vehicle, gets in, then sits down behind the
steering wheel. He starts dozzing-off.)
(Talking to himself, out loud.)

I can't believe that was an angel I just kissed!
Come to think of it...
Molly was always an angel!

      FADE OUT

FADE IN-Night time. Solly , still sitting
behind wheel.
 OFF STAGE: Music, "POEMS"
      SOLLY
Wow! It's dark![Looking at his watch.] I must
have slept a couple of hours. [He turns his head
toward direction of music. The song is "Poems."
He waits a little, then exits vehicle, tip toes
up the stairs, and enters building.
 INTERIOR-Nursing home main lobby
Solly walks toward sound of music, down a long
hallway, which is very dark. This leads him to
the main auditorium. As he approaches the
auditorium door, it is slightly ajar, and a
strong light is shinning through. The music gets
louder and louder, and even more beautiful.

      SOLLY
 Solly peeks into the auditorium.
      [Back shot of entire orchestra. There are

over a hundred senior citizen musicians, all with
white hair, (or maybe they are a hundred coss-
over angels,) all seated and playing on a white
stage, and are all dressed in white formal wear.
There is an accented white glow, created by a
strong white beam of light coming through the
large glass skylight on ceiling.] Solly spots
Molly, seated at a large Grand piano. He then
focuses-in on the back of the conductor. The
conductor slowly turns towards Solly, revealing
that he is GOYSHAN, wearing a white tux, smiling,
with his pulsating white baton in his hand,
wearing a white yamulka.
[Close-up] He reacts to seeing Goyshan, by
opening his eyes wide, then walks over to him].
(Music is lowered here so we can hear
conversation.)

Is that you, Goyshan, or are you (laughing with
trepidation) a cross-over angel too?

        GOYSHAN
[Close-up] He just smiles, and continues to lead
orchestra.

        SOLLY
If you are a cross-over angel, whose cross-over
angel are you?

        GOYSHAN
[Zoom in on half body shot] Smiling, turns his
head towards Solly, then uses his baton (music
comes back to very strong at this point) to point
at SOLLY! (Baton lights up with radiating circles
of light, with accompanying waves of pulsating
sound)
        SOLLY
Solly's mouth slowly opens, and his hand comes
to his mouth.
[Slow fading away shot, on entire auditorium
then up through skylight.]

[TITLES come on with music (Poems) still playing.
Overhead aerial shot looking down through
skylight onto orchestra.]

ADDITIONAL ENDING DURING TITLES

        FADE IN:[Aerial shot of birds flying over
White Lake, then swooping down over Solly's
deck.]

[Close-up on Solly's radio.]

OFF STAGE: RADIO ANNOUNCER
It is my privilege to announce to you, the
winning song of our Mountain Music contest..

[Solly and Goyshan are sitting near radio, very
attentive.]

        SOLLY
[Jumping up and down]
Come on, MOUNTAIN MAN! (Yelling, as if he is at a
race track,coaksing-on his horse.)

        GOYSHAN
[Jumping up and down]
Come on, MOUNTAIN MAN! (In unison with Solly)

        SOLLY
Shoosh! (Putting his finger to his lips!)

        RADIO ANNOUNCER
The winning song writer is a local White Lake
resident, who submitted the following song,
"MOUNTAIN MAN!". Thank you , Solly Batimo! You
have won the five thousand dollars, with your
free trip to Nashville!

        SOLLY
(He is jumping up and down, grabs Goyshan, swings
him around, and they both start dancing to the
music. Solly picks up his guitar, and sings along
with the radio.)

BEFORE TITLES END:

[Close-Up] ON SOLLY and GOYSHAN.

Please don't tell your friends about our SURPRISE ENDING.

        Thank you, thank you!

            END

        (Offstage) Poems Background music.

        FADE OUT to Black Screen,
then Goyshan's animated,white,pulsating baton,jumps out
onto screen, swaying and dancing with the music
        shooting.....

        Large, White Letters on Black Screen.

        MORE... SOLLY, MOLLY, and GOYSHAN in "SNOWBIRDS"
                IN PRODUCTION FOR TV,
                COMING THIS FALL!

            (OFF SCREEN)
            ANNOUNCER (Voice louder than background music)

        MORE... SOLLY, MOLLY and GOYSHAN in "SNOWBIRDS"-
        The EXCITING NEW TV Series.In production! Coming
        this fall.